This book is dedicated to the
2012–2013 Phoenix Five:
Sheridan Spencer,
Andrew Duffy,
Lily Bader-Huffman,
Vanessa Riley,
and Jagger.

Forgive me.

Also by Lisi Harrison

Pretenders
License to Spill

Monster High
Monster High: The Ghoul Next Door
Monster High: Where There's a Wolf, There's a Way
Monster High: Back and Deader Than Ever

Alphas
Movers and Fakers
Belle of the Brawl
Top of the Feud Chain

The Clique
Best Friends for Never
Revenge of the Wannabes
Invasion of the Boy Snatchers
The Pretty Committee Strikes Back
Dial L for Loser
It's Not Easy Being Mean
Sealed with a Diss
Bratfest at Tiffany's
The Clique Summer Collection
P.S. I Loathe You
Boys R Us
Charmed and Dangerous: The Rise of the Pretty Committee
The Cliquetionary
These Boots Are Made for Stalking
My Little Phony
A Tale of Two Pretties

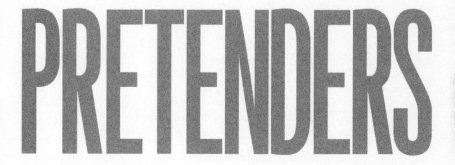

PRETENDERS

BY #1 *NEW YORK TIMES* BESTSELLING AUTHOR
LISI HARRISON

poppy

Little, Brown and Company
New York Boston

Poppy

Hachette Book Group
237 Park Avenue, New York, NY 10017
Visit our website at lb-teens.com

Poppy is an imprint of Little, Brown and Company.
The Poppy name and logo are trademarks of Hachette Book Group, Inc.

The publisher is not responsible for websites (or their content)
that are not owned by the publisher.

First Paperback Edition: May 2014
First published in hardcover in October 2013 by Little, Brown and Company

Library of Congress Cataloging-in-Publication Data

Harrison, Lisi.
Pretenders / by Lisi Harrison. — First edition.
pages cm.
Summary: "Five high school freshmen—the Phoenix Five—reveal their friendships, crushes, school and family dramas, and big secrets, as told in their unique voices through journal entries"— Provided by publisher.
ISBN 978-0-316-22244-0 (hc)—ISBN 978-0-316-22232-7 (pb)
[1. High schools—Fiction. 2. Schools—Fiction. 3. Diaries—Fiction. 4. Friendship—Fiction. 5. Dating (Social customs)—Fiction. 6. Family life—New Jersey—Fiction. 7. New Jersey—Fiction.] I. Title.
PZ7.H2527Pqm 2013 [Fic]—dc23 2012048434

10 9 8 7 6 5 4 3 2 1

RRD-C

Printed in the United States of America

A Foreword by LISI HARRISON

Nickel-colored storm clouds skulked across the sky above Noble High School like timid freshmen. Summer break was over. Notebooks were blank, sneakers were clean, destinies unknown. The seventh annual back-to-school downpour was all that anyone could accurately predict.

Older students, and even some teachers, claimed the rain was actually the evaporated tears of terrified ninth graders. Because in spite of obvious first-day stressors (outfit regret, humidity hair, lame locker location, crush blushing, classroom confusion, lunch tray collisions, and loser abusers), students at Noble High were expected to make like Microsoft and Excel. "Achieve or Leave" was the unofficial motto; the Harvard of High Schools, its unofficial name.

Ranked number one in the country for nearly two decades, the prestigious institution was the reason most families lived in Noble. Without the school, Noble would just be another drive-thru town off I-95, another weed in the Garden State.

Not that it would ever come to that. Scandals destroyed schools, and Noble High didn't do scandals. And yet... in 2013, sometime during Labor Day weekend, that changed.

Students returned from summer vacation to find bound copies of stolen journals propped up against their lockers. Journals written by five freshmen during the previous year. Journals no one was ever supposed to read.

Now the clouds over Noble High will rain tears not just for one day but for many months to come.

♡ Lisi

INTRODUCTION

September 2013

The following journal entries are 100% real and 100% un-edited. I should know. Many of them are mine.

Don't blame Ms. Silver. She meant what she said about wanting us to have a private place to record our feelings; to take a break from screens and reconnect with the written word. She really did lock them up in the teachers' lounge, as promised. If you need to blame someone, blame me.

My picture is on page eighteen of Noble High's 2012–2013 *Phoenix* yearbook. I am one of the PHOENIX FIVE. You nominated me. You thought I was one of the most outstanding students in our freshman class. You were wrong.

Still, I accepted my award. I acted special. But I couldn't help wondering what it would be like if it was for real, if I was actually outstanding. What *do* outstanding people think about? What do they eat for breakfast? Do they worry? Is life easier when you're born with exceptional talent, brains, looks, drive, athleticism, or money? I needed to know. So I broke into the safe and stole all five of our journals.

I'm not exposing them because I'm jealous or I want revenge. I am doing this because I'm tired and I know you are too. The success bar is too high, and pretending has become the only way to reach it. Instagrams are filtered, Facebook profiles are embellished, photos are shopped, reality TV is scripted, body parts get upgraded like software, and even professional athletes are cheating. The things we believe in aren't real. Everyone is a pretender.

The proof is in these pages.

It's time to rise from the ashes of deceit and accept our true selves. To rearrange the letters in Phoenix and become X-Phonies instead. Then, and only then, will we truly know what it feels like to be outstanding.

Welcome to sophomore year,

X-PHONIE

(**X** for short. It's cooler.)

Sheridan

9.4.12

INTERIOR. NOBLE HIGH—ALMOST LUNCHTIME.

A classroom stretches out before us. SHERIDAN
SPENCER, an alluring freshman, sits center row,
center seat. Poised, she click-starts her pen and
writes.

Morning One as a Noble High freshman did not involve a
lot of handholding. Like, none, in fact. Which was fine. It's just
not what I'm used to.

One might assume I do well in new situations because I channel celebrities for confidence. Like, right now for example, I am
pretending to be Blake Lively. But if I'm being totally honest,
which I am, first days are hard no matter how famous you act.

When I (as Blake) arrive someplace new I'm greeted right away. I'm given a tour of the set and offered a Dr Pepper on ice, no straw. My trailer is decorated to my exact specifications; boho-chic and stocked with Original, Tropical, and Sour Skittles. But this morning? Notsomuch. The only rainbow I tasted came from the Lucky Charms burp I tried to suppress at the Pick and Flick. (That's what everyone calls the pickup/drop-off curb.)

FLASHBACK.

It happened as I watched the taillights on my dad's BMW M5 disappear into the morning fog. I was standing with my very best friend, Audri Dunsing. She always rides with me because we live in the same gated community and...well, more on her later. The point is, we were just standing at the Pick and Flick because we didn't know where to go yet. I guess we could have followed everyone else, but we were kind of stunned because our middle school was tiny and this place is huge. Anyway, it's raining and I'm trying to open my zebra umbrella. Backpacks are bashing into us and it's total chaos. O'course, that's when Audri gets a whiff of my burp and decides to shout:

Ewwwwww, Sheridan! Digestive tract issues much?

I managed to apply more Russian Red lipstick, which helped me hold on to a bit of Blake. But not enough. I was seriously mortified. So I go: *Sick! What is that smell?* while fanning the air all innocent. Then I fan-smacked some older Blair Waldorf–type in the neck.

Sorry, it was an accident. (Me.)

You're the accident! (Her.)

Remember those old cartoons where the coyote runs off a cliff and freezes in the air? It isn't until he looks down and realizes he's in trouble that he falls. Well, that's kind of what happened to me when Blair and her friends started laughing. I realized I wasn't really Blake Lively and my confidence took a dive—whistle sound effects and all. Which turned me back into me: Sheridan Spencer, future screen star, including but not limited to TV, film, computer, and tablet. Current blooper.

Anyway, I pull Audri off the main path and onto the grass lawn—which is huge, by the way. As big as Spencer BMW (my dad's dealership), which has, like, hundreds of sedans and SUVs, and I go: *Thanks a lot, Audri!*

O'course she starts speed-blinking and I know exactly where this is going. Yes, I have a stronger stage presence than Audri. (I've played leads in *Wizard of Oz*, *Wicked*, *Annie*, *Mary Poppins*, *Beauty and the Beast*, *Hansel and Gretel*, *High School Musical*, *The Little Mermaid*, *Grease*, and six holiday tributes to the birth of Jesus.) But when it comes to fake crying? She's the best. Our old drama coach called her Meryl Weep.

Why did you call me out on that burp? (Me. Not letting it go.)

Sniffle, sniffle. *I'm sorry.* (Meryl.)

She took off her signature blue-framed glasses, jammed them in the pocket of her Lucky Brand denim jacket, and wiped her wet cheeks. I rolled my eyes.

Watch those tears, little freshman! (Some random blond guy.)

He had choppy layers and blue eyes like Niall Horan from One Direction. But zero of Niall's charm. I'm guessing from his rounded shoulders that he underdelivered on stage presence too. Anyway, after the tears comment he said: *I drove a convertible. If you make it rain I'm going to stuff you in my trunk.* Then he jingled his car keys in Audri's face the way my mom used to do with the twins.

What was that for? (Me, after he left.)

Audri shrugged and put her glasses back on.

FLASHBACK OVER.

Whatever Zero Direction meant about the rain, he was right. It's been pouring for hours. The good news is there have been no further embarrassments. The horrible news is that Audri and I don't have a single class together. Not even lunch. And so far no one has made any effort to meet me. Maybe tomorrow I'll channel a more approachable blonde like Reese Witherspoon.

Ms. Silver just gave us the ten-minute warning. So far she's my favorite teacher. All we've done is write in these journals. She wants us to fill these pages by the end of the year. She swears she won't read them. To prove it she gave us these leather cases with locks on them. She said she'd flip through the journals at the end of the year to make sure they're full but that's it. All she cares about is getting us away from computers. I'm going to record everything and eventually adapt these musings into a one-woman show. I can't wait to tell Audri so she can do it too.

OMG! So the guy beside me is writing with unbridled passion. Hold on. I have to peek.

7

OMG! OMG! I side-eyed him at the exact same time he was side-eyeing me. A simultaneous side-eye. How romantic comedy is *that*? I smiled my eyes into narrow crinkles (like Blake's). I must look fetching in my Russian Red lipstick because he got all nervous and looked away. He appears to be drawing hearts!

Are alleged hearts for me? Is he even cute? I want to peek again but—

The bell.

To Be Continued...

END SCENE.

DUFFY

Tuesday

Andrew Duffy. Andrew Duffy. Andrew Duffy. Andrew Duffy. Andrew Duffy. Andrew Duffy. Andrew Duffy. Every-one calls me Duffy. Duffy. Duffy. Duffy. Duffyyyyyyyyyyy.

Duffy.

Duffy.

Duffy.

Duffy.

Duffy.

Duffy.

Duffy.

Um. Um. Um. Um. Um. Um. Um. Um. Um. Um. Um.
Um. Um. Um. Um. Um. Um. Um. Um. Um. Um. Um.
Um. Um. Um. Um. Um. Um. Um. Um. Um. Um. Um.

How am I supposed to write 250 pages about feelings in one year? Do we even have 250 feelings?

I'd ask Ms. Silver but she said no questions. Just write. Don't worry about spelling or grammar or structure. Just write. She said some other stuff about pressure and being a freshman, but I yawned, and when I yawn I go deaf for a second. So I missed that part. Then she gave out these cases with locks so our thoughts stay private. But the logo on my case is the same as the one on those boxes my sisters jam in the trash. A half-open flower or something.

Uh, Ms. Silver, I don't see how carrying a purse full of feelings is gonna help me deal with being a freshman. It might get me killed, though.

Some skinny dude by the window is drumming on his journal with a pencil. It's kinda annoying and kinda bold cuz it's a major diss to the teacher. She keeps looking up from her laptop but he's not stopping. I bet he's gonna be this year's Class-*ick*. Last year it was Benji Stryker. He stole Hud's DS and offered to sell it back to him for double the price. And Hud actually—

Ms. Silver just busted the drummer. He's wearing this old Rolling Stones concert shirt and she called him Mick. Mostly everyone laughed. I didn't. It would have been cooler if she called him Charlie Watts, cuz Charlie's the drummer in the Stones. The guy does have a Mick thing going on, though, even though the real Mick's hair is brown and the Class-*ick*'s is auburn. (I know that means reddish-brown because my sister Mandy is always stinking up the bathroom with her "auburn" hair color kits.) But their cuts are similar. You know, long and choppy. And he's got that frog face girls would like if he was famous. Anyway, he stopped pencil drumming, so that's good.

I want to look behind me and see what Coops is doing so I will. I will look behind me and see what Coops is doing. One, two, three . . .

I just saw Coops's scalp. Either he has lice or dandruff because there were these white specks in his hair. His head is down like he's taking a test. What is he writing about? Our other buddy Hudson is in a different class. Which is fine, I guess. We'll all be on the basketball team together. I can't wait for tryouts. Playing Varsity is going to be so cool.

Now what? Now what?

Now what?

Now what?

NOW WHAT?

Those <u>What I Did Over Summer Vacation</u> essays were cool because I got to write the same thing every year.

1. Listen to my older sisters fight.
2. Basketball camp.
3. Shoot hoops with Coops and Hud after camp so I don't have to listen to my older sisters fight.

4. Go on a boys-only fly-fishing trip with my dad so
   we don't have to listen to my older sisters fight.

My essay was in paragraph form, but I decided to write it this way because numbering takes up more space.

Duffy. Duffy has the ball. Duffy is on fire. Duffy is unstoppable. Duffy shoots the winning basket!

Woo-hooooooooooooooooooooooooooooooooooooooooooooooooo oooooooooooooooooooooooooooooooooooooooooooooooooooooooo oooooooooooooooooooooooooooooooooooooooooooooooooooooooo oooooooooooooooooooooooooooooooooooooooooooooooooooooooo ooooooooo

Some girl in a yellow dress saw me making those o's. Then she smiled. She has red lipstick on her tooth. I turned away really fast like I had some big feeling that needed to be written down. And now I'm just writing and writing to look busy. I hope someone tells her about her tooth. It looks like blood but I know it's not, because my Bubbie Libby gets that all the time.

Bubbie is what Jewish people call their grandmothers. We're not Jewish. But Bubbie Libby is. She converted when my grandfather died because she thinks Jewish men are good listeners, and she wants to die knowing what it feels like to have a real conversation. So she lives with us and waits for the Chosen One. Whatever that's about.

Maybe I'll email Amelia tonight. She got a scholarship to an all girls college in New York. She's into poetry and women's rights and talking about girl things that me and my dad do

NOT want to hear about. She's smart with journals and has tons of them locked in a safe. Like anyone would ever want to read this stuff.

The bell.

— LATER

Jagger

Sept. 4.

Feelings? Get real. I stopped having feelings on February 13, 2012—the day my parents got tossed in jail.

I've been emancipated since I was fourteen.

I'm fifteen now.

I live alone.

I take care of myself.

I don't have time for feelings.

My name is Jagger.

I don't even have time for a last name.

-J

Lily

Tuesday, September 4, 2012

My name is Lily, I turn fifteen next month, and I am eating for three. Wait, I think it's four if you kount me, and ready for this: Mom and Dad are klueless kuz I still look way-skinny. Thank you, Karess.

Not only is Karess a personal trainer slash DJ, he is the father of my triplets. He's into spelling C words with K's so now I am too.

Back to my skinnyness.

Karess recommended protein bars and energy drinks to keep the baby weight off, and ready for this: Five months pregnant and I've already lost 11 pounds. Kan you believe?

Once I "show" we'll Greyhound it to L.A. and open a gym called Kut. It will kost a million dollars to join so we kan get rich in one day. Karess wants to name the kids Karb, Kalorie, and Kardio. Luv it. Luv him. Luv the kreativity.

School is for unpregnant losers. Like what's the point of this journal assignment if I'm going to open a gym? Also my hand is shaking kuz I've had seven energy drinks on an empty stomach. Well, empty of food, not triplets. Point is it's hard to write.

Klass is over! Next stop, kemistree.

Lily

Tuesday, September 4, 2012
(Midnight)

I left my journal on the kitchen table for six whole hours. Mom made two attempts to bust the lock, first at 4:27 PM and again at 7:19 PM, but she couldn't guess my combo (A.D.'s b-day). Even if she did, and then managed to hide the clues, I'd know. That fake entry about Karess would shock her blind. She'd circle the living room like a mad cow, slamming into bookcases, knocking over newspaper stacks, tripping on lamp cords. Believe me, I'd know.

Thanks to this sturdy locking mechanism, I can be free. Free to discover the real Lily Bader-Huffman. Not the A+ student, with the male best friend, who has been homeschooled

for eight years. The one who is forming beneath her. Growing like a shadow. Faceless and distorted; elongating and reaching; determined to make her secret dream come true. Determined to be normal and popular and kissed by—

Uh-oh . . . footsteps.

Lily Bader-Huffman Version 2.0

Vanessa

September 4th

The English assignment given by Ms. Silver on September 4, 2012, @ 1:47 PM is as follows: Each student must record his or her innermost thoughts and feelings during freshman year at Noble High. The goal is to have a safe place to connect with ourselves. The challenge will be finding our voices and the courage to embrace them. These journals will not be graded or read. Ms. Silver will inspect them at the end of the year to make sure we filled all 250 pages. That is it. We will also have to write an essay about self-discovery and what we learned. But we are not supposed to focus on that now.

At 1:49 PM I inquired as to whether we would benefit by

filling additional journals. To which she responded, "Not in the form of grades." To which I asked, "Will our GPAs benefit?" To which she replied, "No. Your soul will." To which I thought, *Forget it, then.*

Thusly, my strategy moving forward is to pen one journal's worth of "innermost thoughts and feelings" while focusing primarily on reward-based endeavors. I will, however, transcribe all feelings and thoughts associated with said endeavors here. Since that's the whole point of this exercise.[1]

I will commence with a brief character profile.

My name is Vanessa Charlot[2] Riley. I am fourteen. My hair is light brown and as curly as an old-fashioned telephone cord.[3] I have green eyes and caramel-colored skin. My mother hails from Haiti, my father Queens. I'm told I look like a much, much, much younger Vanessa Williams.[4] Better than Venus Williams. Ha.

As columnist Gina Simmons from the *Noble High Times* put it, "Exotic and striking, even Vanessa's features overachieve." My middle school principal signed my yearbook with, "Beauty and Brains, you are proof that girls can have both."

....

[1] That was a sentence fragment. I will leave it because Ms. Silver told us to ignore grammar. Please don't penalize me.

[2] Pronounced Shar-low. It's my mother's maiden name. It's Creole, based largely on 18th-to-21st-century French.

[3] Simile.

[4] Circa 1983, when she won Miss America (except my hair is shoulder-length, clavicle-length when wet or flat-ironed).

I prefer using quotes to characterize myself for three reasons:

1) Quotes prove opinions.
2) No one likes a gloater.
3) I must be liked.

My favorite hobby is winning.[5] The endorphins feed my heart and carbonate my blood. It's a euphoric rush, but it ends as soon as I get my prize. The only way to get it back is to win again. I compare it to the ever-stale Bazooka bubble gum— tough work for a moment of sweetness. But, oh, how sweet that moment is. Hence, the reason I'm always chasing that next piece.

Well, it's half the reason.

Veritas[6]? It goes deeper than endorphins and carbonated blood. I'm just not sure how to explain it, since "it" is more of a feeling than an actual thing.

Actually, it's fragments of a feeling. Fleeting fragments like scattered dandelion fluff. Fuzzy bits drift by but I've never

---

[5] I currently have 159 awards. (Complete list available upon request.) I have served as student council president for three consecutive years. I was captain of the eighth-grade track-and-field team. I have been a Girl Scout for seven years. I have never received a grade lower than A.
[6] Latin for "truth."

tried to grab them or piece them into thoughts. Maybe because thinking them in full would make them real. And I don't want them to be real because they have to do with my parents.[7]

But Ms. Silver asked for innermost so I'm going to connect the fuzzy bits and tell you what I try not to think about. Ready?

It's my parents. How much they fight. And why that affects my grades and wardrobe.

This morning began with a screaming match about my older brother, A.J.[8] Then it became about Dad and how he'd rather dissect computers than listen to stories about Mom's evil boss at the hotel. Which transitioned into the things Mom flushes down the toilet. Nothing says "Good luck on your first day of high school" like an argument about clogged pipes.

I'm never involved in these squabbles but I am allergic to conflict, so I suffer. Veritas? Fighting sounds make me itchy. I have red marks all over my arms and legs to prove it. Like I was jumped by the Real Housewives of New Jersey on Acrylic Day.

Peers assume I'm modest because I wear long sleeves to keep from scratching. Modesty on a girl with features that

---

[7] I just took a pause. I'm starting to fatigue from the surge of heavy emotions gathering in my hands.

[8] A.J. failed eleventh grade and has to repeat it this year. He's always getting suspended and he's really disrespectful to Mom and Dad. The only things he cares about are cars. So they never let him drive one.

"overachieve" does make her more likable, so it's not all bad. But it's not all good, either. Obvious frump factor aside, running track in sweats leads to heatstroke. In 98 percent humidity, hallucinations. But it's worth it. First place means my parents will stay together another day. So I cover up and run like a nose in flu season.

You see, every time I get an A, or win something, or am elected, crowned, honored, published, or profiled, we celebrate at Benihana.[9] A.J. and I can order anything we want. Wear whatever we want. We're even allowed to get double desserts. The only thing we can't do at Beni's is fight. It's our family rule. And it sticks like chewed Bazooka.

In summation: Overachieving = Benihana = Peace = No divorce.

Simple.

If you focus on success, you'll have stress. But if you pursue excellence, success will be guaranteed.

—Deepak Chopra[10]

---

[9] Best tempura! The same rule applies to A.J., only he's never won anything. So it's all on me.

[10] Inspirational quotes are my caffeine. Same with caramel lattes from Starbucks.

Jagger

Sept. 4.

One more thing.

A FemFresh case with a lock is not gonna happen.
I'd rather hide my journal in dirty boxer shorts.
Safer that way.
Less embarrassing too.

-J

Lily

Wednesday, September 5, 2012

Blake rode over before school this morning to give me a dozen yellow roses.

"Yellow signifies new beginnings," he said, one foot still on his skateboard.

I flicked his cheek, which was always tanned, even in December. "I know what yellow means."

He smiled. "I owe you, big-time. If there's ever anything you need—"

"Yeah, yeah."

We stood there for a minute. Him with his wet black hair and me with a glob of syrup on my denim skirt, remembering the day we decided to go for it. I know he was thinking about it too because Blake has been my best friend for eight years and we know everything about each other.

The public school thing came up for the first time in June. We were coming back from Six Flags when his mom said she had to go back to work in the fall. Translation? After eight years of homeschooling, Blake would have to go to Noble.

The news gave him a crazy asthma attack. Which always makes me cry. And when I cry, Mom cries. Then Mrs. Marcus started because she felt responsible. She said she had no choice because they needed the money. Still, Blake kept right on wheezing.

Like me, Blake loved being a Homie (our slang for home-schoolers) and did not want to be a Pub boy (slang for public schooler). He loved thumbing his nose at the mainstream. And loved that our moms taught us together. He couldn't stand Pub drama and was afraid he'd get mixed up in it. But I knew the truth. Blake was afraid people would pick on him because he's gay.

I reminded him that New Jersey is a blue state and, anyway, Noble kids are too intelligent for ignorant behavior, but he kept quoting statistics from a survey that said being gay was the number two reason kids get bullied.

"What's number one?" I asked.

"Appearance."

"Then I have more to worry about than you," I said.

"Moot," Blake snipped. "You're not being sent to Pub. I am."

So I asked my parents if I could go to Pub too.

They said no.

I appealed with a seven-page essay on the benefits of diversifying my education. I set up a tour of the school. Blake pulled the stats on what percentage of Noble grads went to Ivy League colleges. It was 47 percent. They caved.

On one condition: I have to maintain my A+ average. If not, I'm back home.

Blake and I laughed at that one. Not succeed at Pub? With *my* education? Failing would be harder.

Once the news was official, Blake began wheezing in a good way. He couldn't believe I did something so selfless. He promised he'd make it up to me. I told him that wasn't necessary because that's what best friends do. I didn't tell him about A.D., though. Better that he thought I was doing it all for him.

I put the roses inside, yelled goodbye to my mom, and grabbed my red board.

Yesterday, the human traffic was so overwhelming we skipped the afternoon and hung at the mall. Which, ironically, wound me up even more. Teenaged mannequins were everywhere, layered and scarved and effortlessly stylish. Not a single one wore a syrup-stained jean skirt. Yes, I wore it two days in a row. It's the cutest thing I have.

So today, we skateboarded up to school late to avoid the crowds. Holding hands, Blake and I inched down the school path with trepidation, like Dorothy and the Cowardly Lion approaching the Wizard.

"Freeze!" called a man as we pushed through the arched doors.

We froze.

The stranger gave us tardy slips and a smug grin, as if those pink papers would show us a thing or two. We didn't care. We were relieved to have the hallway to ourselves.

Our damp Chucks squeaked against the checkerboard-tiled floors as he Dorothied and I Lioned our way to class. We passed rooms full of strangers, muffled voices of teachers, sentinels of sticker-covered lockers, vending machines, cafeteria smells, and multi-stalled bathrooms. Nothing *Teen Vogue* or *Seventeen* has written could ever have prepared me for this sensorial barrage.

"This is so weird." I giggled. "We're actually in Pub. Think we'll make it through day two?"

"Get to class!" shouted Tardy Slip.

"Nope," Blake whispered.

"You owe me," I whispered.

"I know."

So far so good, though. It's last period and I'm still here. I'm in Algebra, zoning because this stuff is so easy. I'm writing so it looks like I'm taking notes.

I still haven't told Blake my secret reason for wanting to go to Noble. A reason that has nothing to do with friendship, diversity, prestige, or Ivy. And everything to do with the boy next door.

His name is Andrew Duffy. He has dirty blond hair, green eyes, full lips, and a space between his teeth. Tall and slender, he walks with a slight forward lean. When he's not dribbling a basketball, his hands are in his pockets. He wears hoodies and uses the hoods. Right now he is copying equations off the board. Watching him feels like skateboarding down a winding hill.

Lily Bader-Huffman-Duffy

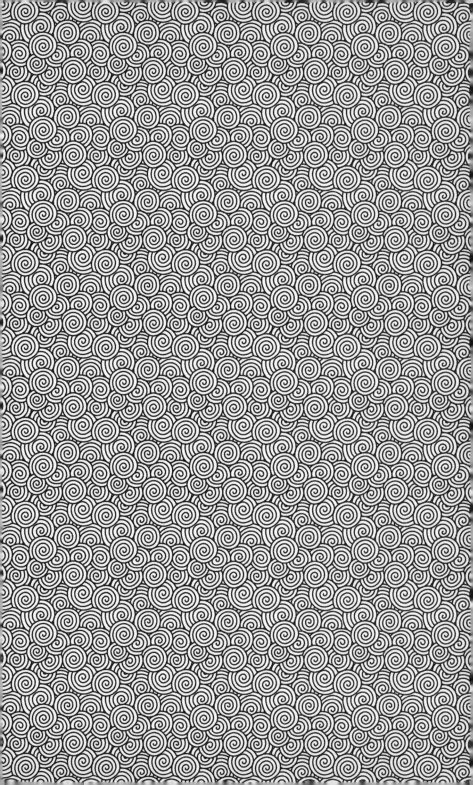

Sheridan

9.5.12

INT. SHERIDAN—NIGHT.

Lavender-scented bath oil glistens off SHERI-DAN's skin. She twists damp hair into a towel-turban, flops down on her Broadway Lights duvet cover, and waits for "Good Morning Baltimore" (*Hairspray* Original Broadway Cast Recording) to fill her earbuds. It does. She writes.

Audri and I went to the mall after school today to shop for back-to-school costumes. We call clothes "costumes" to feel more like actresses. Which we are. The only difference is I eat, breathe, and sleep the craft whereas Audri just breathes it. But it works. She's been my understudy for seven plays in a row. Eight, once they cast the freshman play.

I hope it's a real drama and not some middle school number like *Annie*. I'm ready to stray from my comfort zone and play "down and out." An outcast with a haunting solo. OMG, Éponine from *Les Mis* would be ideal. I've never been "troubled" before, and I've never channeled a depressed celebrity, so it would be a challenge. One I am ready to embrace.

Anyway, back to the mall. I have a modest chest, flat abs, and a Rubenesque undercarriage. I know it's pointless to be upset about things you can't change, especially body parts, and double-especially healthy ones. But according to the Old Navy denim bar, I'm a "pear." And let's be honest, there aren't a ton of leading roles for pears. So I left in a huff without trying anything on.

Audri said I could try out for a Fruit of the Loom commercial. We cracked up all the way to Jamba Juice. Then I got upset again because that place is all fruit and I felt mocked.

While browsing at Forever 21, Audri said there are a lot of ample-bottomed stars, like Jennifer Lopez, Jessica Biel, Maria Menounos, and the Dove models. She offered to trade bodies with me because she's a "celery." She dangled her skinny arms by her shapeless hips to prove it.

Curves are sexy. (Audri. Suddenly an authority.) *Trust me, Sher, boys prefer pears to celeries.*

Why?

More to sink their teeth into.

I practically choked on my Five Fruit Frenzy because just as she was saying that, three semi-hotties walked by and heard the whole thing.

When did you become such an expert? I wanted to ask, but didn't. (It felt so good to be back at the mall laughing with Audri, I didn't want to ruin the moment.)

Audri and I have been sole mates since first grade. FYI, that was not a spelling mistake. We call each other *sole* mates because yes, we are soul mates, but we are also *sole* mates because we're all we need.

She spent all summer at sleepaway camp because her parents were going through a divorce and they needed "space." It felt like my entire left side was missing. I worked at Retirement Village to stay busy. You'd be surprised how much money you can earn reading books to the elderly. I made $475 and an extra $63 in tips because I made an effort to enunciate and used a different voice for each character.

So I had all this cash and Audri had guilt money from her mother so we loaded up the dressing room with colorful skinny jeans. This o'course made me crave Skittles, which reminded me of tasting the rainbow, which made me think of my Lucky Charms burp, which flashed me back to the first day of school. I asked Audri what she thought of Noble so far.

It's kinda hard.

I know. I already have math homework and a social studies essay due Monday.

Same.

We should get glasses at CVS and channel Alex from Modern Family.

I was expecting Audri to say "same" again because she always agrees with me. But she said, *I'd rather be Haley because she gets tons of guys and Noble has mucho cute ones.*

Any One Direction-ers? (Harry Styles is my favorite.)

Hundreds. Audri checked her celery butt in the three-way mirror. *I need tighter.*

It was totally weird to hear her say that because Audri has never really talked about boys or tight clothes like that before. I wanted to ask her if she learned it from sleepaway camp but I didn't want to sound like a prude so I told her about the guy in my English class who was looking at me and drawing hearts.

Babe? (Audri.)

The talking pig?

No. Babe as in cute. Is he cute?

I guess. (Me. Annoyed that I'm having a hard time zipping up a pair of red skinny jeans.)

Cute enough for tongue?

Audri!!!

Well?

He's kinda shy.

That means he likes you.

You mean he likes pears. (Me, kicking off the tight jeans and cursing my Rubenesque undercarriage.)

Audri gripped my chin and turned my head to face the mirror.

Sheridan Spencer, you are super hot and everyone knows it. Wavy blond hair, caramel eyes, zero blemishes. Guys always check you out and you always get the lead in plays. And it's, like, impossible for you to look ugly in a head shot.

I Mona Lisa smiled at my reflection. Audri was right about one thing: The lens loves my flat round face. Audri, who is more on the pointy side, thinks she photographs like a rodent. Templeton from *Charlotte's Web* to be specific, especially when the camera gives her red-eye. I still think she's pretty in an Emma Watson kind of way.

I wanted to ask her why my ratings are so low this season. Or why no one is making an effort to talk to me if I'm so "super hot." But Mrs. Levinsky at Retirement Village said low self-esteem gives women wrinkles. And that a performer with my abilities should *act* confident when she doesn't feel it. She made me promise not to put myself down and then passed, like, two days later. So I held my tongue in honor of her dying wish.

Anyone cool in your classes? (Me. While Audri is paying for a see-through tank top even though winter is on the way and it's been raining for days.)

There's this one guy in American History. I think his name is Jagger . . .

Reddish-brown hair? Thin? Indie band-ish? Yeah, we're in English together.

I heard his parents are on death row.

What? Why?

Not sure yet. But I do know he lives alone and is allowed to sign his own report cards. I'd say that makes him "cool."

I guess.

I should sit with him at lunch one day.

What about girls? Any cool ones?

A few have introduced themselves but . . . I dunno, Noble is kinda different. It's like everyone is more into the school part of school than the fun part.

Exactly. (Yay. She hadn't met anyone she liked yet either.)

Where to now?

I shrugged because I really didn't know. All I wanted to do was go home and journal. Weird, I know. But it's what I was feeling so I owned it. Oprah would have been proud.

On the ride home Audri and I agreed that if we did everything together like carpool, study, act, and have sleepovers on the weekends she's not in Montclair with her dad, we wouldn't feel so separated. Audri even suggested we leave secret notes for each other in the cafeteria since she has early lunch and I have late. How cute is that?

The mall was great even though I didn't buy anything. The plans I made with Audri helped me feel better than a thousand costumes ever could.

END SCENE.

41

DUFFY

Friday

I'm in my room waiting to Skype Amelia. I've been trying to get in touch with her for three days so she could tell me how to write about feelings. But she's been too busy with college and needed to "set a time." Friday at 6:40 PM is our "time." I swear. She can be so—

Okay, just got off Skype. For someone so "busy" she certainly had "time" to bore me with the differences between the female and male brain and how we "process emotions." Can't she just answer the question?

This was me: Hey A, I'm supposed to write 250 pages about my feelings. What do I do?

This was her: Oh, wow! How cool. Who is the teacher? Is she new? Sorry. That was wrong of me to assume she's a woman. But something tells me she is. Is she? (I nod that she is. Amelia looks proud of herself). Journaling should be mandatory in high school, especially for boys. They have such a hard time expressing (yawn = deaf)...think about Dad and...(yawn = deaf)...Andrew stop yawning, it's rude... this is crucial...manage stress...reduce the risk of heart attack...(bored = deaf)...not to mention a better husband and father, especially to young...

Mom's calling me for dinner.

That was me interrupting because my legs were getting restless.

Any tips? You know, on how to do it? What do I talk about?

HER: Write about the most important thing that happens to you each day and how it makes you *feeeeel*. Once you get more comfortable with that process we can take it further, more along the lines of—

ME: Coming, Mom! Gotta go. Thanks, Amelia. Love ya.

Amelia is super smart but she's so serious. Then there's Mandy, who's way more into her slick boyfriend Gardner and fashion and stuff. She's cool too but they're both kind of annoying. I would never hang out with a girl like Amelia or Mandy. It would be cool to find one who's a mix of both, smart and into girl stuff. A sister-mutt.

Anyway, I got Amelia's point. Write about the most important things that happen each day and how they made me feel. So here's today.

School dragged.

Had lunch with Hud, Coops, and four girls who whispered and giggled.

Six more days until basketball tryouts.

No hoops after school again because it's raining.

Feeling = Bored.

Bubbie Libby said we should gather the animals and build an ark. I'll donate the two Malteses Mom bought to replace Amelia. We've had them for three weeks. All they do is yap and poop on the carpet in the TV room. Mandy won't walk them in the rain because she got a blowout. My parents can't because they work late. Bubbie says low air pressure gives her joint pain. And I refuse to walk dogs that wear matching outfits and pink hair bows. Besides, I still don't know their names. One day it's Maybelline and Revlon. Then it's Vanilla and Blanca or Ellen and Portia. No one can agree. I told Dad we shouldn't name them anything. That way when no one is talking they'll think we're calling them and they'll come. Dad said someone is always talking in this house so that would never work. He's right.

Rosie our cleaning woman used to walk the dogs but she doesn't work here anymore. Mom said she quit to spend more time with her kids. Bubbie did that fake cough thing to let me know Mom was lying. Then Mom said: Really, Mother? and left the kitchen. Whatever. I don't need to know why Rosie left. I just wish she was still here to clean the Tootsie Rolls. Mom makes me do it or I can't play Wii.

Feeling = Over the rain.

Mom is calling me for real this time. We have a Jewish Sabbath dinner every Friday for Bubbie. Mandy used to complain about it because it messed up date night with Gardner. Dad and I weren't into it because we like to get Italian takeout and watch sports. But Mom said Bubbie isn't going to be around forever and we should do this for her. So we compromised. Mandy gets to bring Gardner and we still get the takeout. We just have to light special candles and eat at the table and not in the TV room, which is fine because there's probably poop in there.

Feeling = Hungry.

I'm back. I've been writing a lot tonight cuz I have a lot to catch up on. Hud is already on page 40. He's been writing about the girls in our grade and what he thinks they eat for breakfast. He says it can tell you a lot about a person. Like this super-smart girl Vanessa. Hud thinks she scarfs a chocolate donut and a Monster Energy drink. He wrote crayons for that girl Sheridan but that's only because I told him about her lipstick tooth. He originally assigned her key lime pie flavored yogurt. The whole thing is kind of weird and kind of funny. So is Hud.

Feeling = Ha.

Coops is on page 63. That's because his parents give him a dollar for every page he writes. They love paying him to do things no one should get paid for. Like making his bed or not choking his brother. He's writing out the words to every Bruce Springsteen song and saving for an electric guitar.

Feeling = No fair.

Anyway, Sabbath dinner tonight was lame because Mom tried to cook. When I asked what happened to the Italian takeout, Bubbie Libby did that cough thing again. Mom and Dad looked at each other, then Mom said she wanted to try something different. She went on and on about how life is about new experiences and breaking routines. After like, ten minutes, I still had no clue what happened to the takeout. Why can't girls just answer the question?

Feeling = Frustrated.

She microwaved frozen chicken nuggets with cheddar sauce and pasta Alfredo from a bag. Bubbie wouldn't eat because she said it wasn't kosher.

MOM: That's because we're not Jewish. Besides, Italian takeout isn't kosher either.

BUBBIE: But it's good so God makes an exception.

MANDY: We serve this to the homeless on Thanks-giving.

GARDNER: I think it's delicious, Mrs. Duffy.

The guy will eat anything as long as it's free. Probably because he wastes his money on slick designer clothes.

Dad and I fed the dogs under the table. Bubbie Libby saw what we were doing and started doing it too.

While we were clearing the table Dad asked me how Hudson's parents are doing.

Dad and Mom sell commercial real estate. Stuff like malls and stores. Hudson's dad does the same thing. They are competitors. But it's all good.

ME: Fine, I guess.

DAD: Good.

That was it. Easy.

Feeling = Glad Dad's a guy.

— LATER

Jagger

Sept. 8.

Finally, a break in the rain. The sky is greenish-black so it's going to get worse.

I am sitting on a cement bench in Regal Park watching some guys shoot hoops.

They don't seem to mind the puddles. It must be nice to love something enough not to mind the puddles.

Two of them are in my English class but don't notice me. Maybe they're pretending because my journal is wrapped in boxer shorts.

I hate the weekend.

Forty-eight hours of nothing to do.

No parents. No siblings. No DS. No TV. No sports. No sleepovers. No Boy Scouts. No cul-de-sac. No friends.

Maybe one day.

Noble is cool.

It's all about achievements. Not mommy and daddy's bank account or who's dancing with who at so-and-so's boy-girl party.

I've been invited to lunch nine different times this week. That's nine times more than Sagewood, and I was sentenced to that place for two years.

That middle school was full of spoiled rich kids who couldn't understand the heavy stuff going on in my life. Not that they ever tried. To them, heavy was an extra pound some cheerleader gained over Christmas vacation.

Do you know how many dog biscuits I eat to gain one pound?

Sixty-three.

Fattening up on Santa-shaped shortbread cookies would be a dream. Not an excuse to starve myself until Valentine's Day.

But that's where my parents had me.

Until they were arrested.

After that I was free to move to a new district and start fresh.

Not that I am any different at Noble. I'm used to keeping to myself so that's how I am.

The one-name thing has been attracting a lot of attention, especially from girls.

They come up to me all squirmy and shoulder-to-shoulder and ask if "Moves Like Jagger" is about me.

Since that song came out last summer and I'm fifteen I invite them to do the math.

Next they ask if I'm trying to be famous and one-name-ish like Bono or Xzibit.

I look at them like a joke I don't get.

I say I'm not trying to be famous at all. I'm trying to survive.

They laugh again but with less of a smile. There's a bigger story here and they sense it might not be pretty. They peer down the hall, or around the classroom, or wherever we are, wanting out.

There's always a brave one who asks what I mean by "survive."

I tell her I'm legally separated from my parents because they're in prison. Last names are for families. I live alone.

They ask me to lunch.

They ask me questions.

I answer them.

Q: Do you seriously live alone?
A: Yes.

Q: Like alone, alone?
A: Alone, alone.

Q: Where?
A: The back room of REP's.

Q: Randy's Exotic Pets?
A: Yup.

Q: Really?
A: Really.

Q: Why?
A: I feed the animals at night and Randy lets me sleep there for free.

Q: I was just there on Saturday! My brother got a skink.
A: They eat baby food, you know.

Q: And spiders. I didn't see you there. Were you there?
A: I leave during store hours. Randy uses the back room, where I sleep, to meet with international pet dealers. Now, those are some shady dudes.

Q: Where do you go?
A: I visit my parents in jail. I hop a train to Manhattan sometimes. When it's cold I read at the public library.

(Silence.)

Q (The Brave One): So, why exactly are your parents in jail?
A: Bully beating.

Q: You mean they beat up bullies?
A: Yup.

Q: Like bullies who were bullying you?

A: No. Not me. Do I look like the kind of guy who gets bullied?

Q: So...?

A: We lived next door to a kid who got picked on. Not in a regular way. This was really bad. Don't ask me for details because I don't like to talk about it. *(The girls look at each other all creeped out and stuff.)* The guy lived with his grandfather who was too old to do anything so he asked my parents if they would, you know, help out.

Q: Did they?

A: Yeah. They kind of overdelivered.

Q: Did you help them?

A: No. I had no clue.

Q: How did you find out?

A: The police came to the door while my mom was making pancakes. A social worker took me and...can we change the subject?

Q: Definitely.

Q: Totally.

Q: Let's.

Q: So what's jail like?

A: It's bad. Really bad. I'd rather spend the day with Mr. Wiggons.

This kills them because Brit Lit is the most boring class at Noble. And Wiggons's cockney accent makes it impossible to understand the boring things he's saying.

Since we're all laughing, everyone in the cafeteria checks us out. They wonder what could possibly be so funny. They wish they were in on it.

No one has actually told me this, but I know. I have seen a lot of things. Dark things. And I have read hundreds of crime novels. If there's one thing I understand it's human behavior.

It's starting to rain again.

Maybe I'll steal a bike.

-J

Lily

Saturday, September 8, 2012

Poor Duffy. You're drenched. You are spinning a basketball on your finger as you walk to your front door. Come over here instead. Let me dry you. Let's spend the afternoon together.

Hot chocolate and Chinese checkers? Fuzzy socks and footsie? Swap sections of the *New York Times*?

You just went in but then opened the door twenty seconds later and tossed the basketball onto the soggy lawn. You don't know that my bedroom window faces the side of your house. You don't know that I have been watching you since you moved next door last spring. I will wait ten minutes, scamper out in the rain, and claim my prize.

Don't be afraid. I'm not psycho. Just homeschooled. I'm still having a hard time getting used to being in the real world. Pub girls get so dressed up. The boys don't sit still. Teachers are serious. Bells are loud. Changing classes is Penn Station on a Friday afternoon. And, worst of all, you have no idea who I am. Someday you will.

Until then...

Lily Bader-Huffman-Duffy

Sheridan

9.9.12

INT. VANILLA-SCENTED BUBBLE BATH—AFTERNOON.

SHERIDAN rests her journal on a white towel in the corner of her bathtub. She opens to a fresh page, closes her eyes, and summons her muse.

Random images cyclone through her mind's eye....Chasing her brothers through Target...A red ballet flat stepping in tar...Biting a burning hot mozzarella stick...Audri feeding Skittles to Harry Styles...SHERIDAN opens her eyes, shakes the bubbles off her right hand, and begins.

I have flu-like symptoms. My body aches and I feel dizzy. I'm not sick, though. Just depressed. Not in a need-meds kind of way. More like I'm buried under a quilt of sadness. It's so cumbersome I can barely lift my quill.

CUT.

Writing the word "quill" just made me smile. Audri always laughs when I call pens "quills."

I miss Audri.

(Sigh.)

Sad again.

SHERIDAN's JOURNAL ENTRY TAKE TWO.

ACTION.

Audri is visiting her dad in Montclair. This divorce is killing me. The good news is, with Audri gone and no rehearsals (yet) I had plenty of time to write my social studies essay this weekend. *That's* my good news. Pathetic, right?

I had to spend the day with my family yesterday because Spencer BMW is selling Mini Coopers now so there was a big party. It was called the Big Mini. Dad made me watch Henry and Max so he and Mom could mingle. It would have been more fun if I had someone to hang out with.

H&M spent most of the day hiding in cars and were taken on three test drives by accident. When Dad found out, he dragged us into that office with all the keys and started lecturing us on respecting the family business. Then a flatbed truck pulled up and he bolted. Saved by the arrival of the BMW M3 GTR! Dad is the first dealer in the tristate area to get the new one and he's been talking it up for, like, ever. So I guess something worked out for me. But that was about it.

(Heavy sigh.)

The bath is getting cold.

I seriously cannot believe no one has tried to friend me. I'm like Beemer, the balloon stick figure outside the dealership who spends his life alone, flapping in the breeze.

I could call the girls from my old drama club. We could see a movie or—

Nah.

They'll ask how Noble is and I'll have to lie and say I've made tons of friends. Then Beemer will flop back into my head and I'll feel more pathetic than I already do. Besides, feeling sorry for myself is no way to honor Mrs. Levinsky. I need to act positive.

CUT.

SHERIDAN's JOURNAL ENTRY TAKE THREE.

ACTION.

I just rolled back my shoulders and pulled the plug with renewed purpose. Water, soiled with self-pity, now drains from my bath. I'm getting cold. I could get out but I have decided to sit with this uncomfortable feeling. It reminds me that life isn't always vanilla-scented and warm. And when it's not we have to rise up from the bubbles and find new ways to smell like cupcakes.

So I shall...

(Freezing.)

Tomorrow I will shine like the top of the Chrysler Building!

(Shivering.)

I will channel a character of great strength and determination! One who refuses to lose or live life unnoticed...(The goose bumps on my legs have sprouted stubble.) A girl with the flair for fabulous and the drive to survive...

Shivering, SHERIDAN hurries from the bath and towels off. She moisturizes, wraps herself in a stolen Four Seasons robe, and contemplates Monday's character.

Strength...Determination...Drive...Flair...Got it! I will wear a fashion-forward costume. I will stockpile witty comebacks. I will cast a Pretty Committee. I will over-gloss and under-smile.

I will channel Massie Block from that straight-to-DVD movie *The Clique*, and I will be ah-mazing.

To Be Continued...

END SCENE.

Vanessa

September 9th

Orange light lingers in the sky as another weekend sets with the sun.[11]

Instead of organizing binders and drafting my goals for the week ahead,[12] I sit crisscross applesauce on the sloping roof of our modest Victorian home. I am wearing a pink racer-back tank and gray drawstring pajama bottoms. My arms are soothed by a mixture of cloves, juniper berries, and oatmeal. A

---

[11] Sentences like this make me wish this journal were being graded.

[12] I do this while eating arrowroot cookies and sipping chamomile tea. Yum.

hungry yellow-headed bird keeps trying to peck me. I am shooing it away with hands covered in dishwashing gloves.

If I wasn't me and saw me, I would speed-dial Noble Psychiatric and have me committed. Ironically, this is all I can do to stay sane.[13]

They almost made it two days without a fight. Granted, Mom was in the city,[14] Dad was at a software convention,[15] and A.J. worked a double at the car wash.[16] Still, I didn't itch once. It was epidermal bliss.

Leena and Megan from Girl Scouts came over to see the prototype for my SWAP bracelet.[17] It's better than I imagined. Orphans follow direction really well. I could have all 500 sold

---

[13] ... and keep from scratching.

[14] She is the concierge at The Lux, a five-star hotel in Manhattan.

[15] Sounds boring, but he loves that stuff.

[16] He owes my parents $800.00 for trashing the side-view mirror on the Audi. He's not allowed to use their car until his debt is paid. The guy is obsessed with driving, so it's killing him.

[17] I entered the Girl Scouts' Young Women of Distinction contest. First place: Gold Award! Super prestigious. My entry is a Sealed With A Promise, or SWAP, bracelet with an envelope charm. You open the flap and whisper a personal message to yourself, then seal it shut. If you want to change it, just open the flap to let out the old one and whisper something new. The bracelets are made by Haitian orphans. All proceeds go to their orphanage. I got the sample on Saturday. I'll take orders Monday.

by the end of the month. Especially since Leena and Megan go to different schools and they'll be selling too.

I digress... the point is, everything was great until dinner, when A.J. announced he got fired.

Again.

He hacked into his boss's computer and changed the wallpaper from a family picture in Nantucket to a naked girl lying on a gondola in Venice. The boss's wife and kids stopped by to bring him lunch and were the first ones to notice it.

Everyone knew A.J. did it because he's a genius with computers. So that was it. The fourth job he lost this year.

Mom blamed Dad for teaching A.J. how to hack. Dad blamed Mom for blaming him instead of A.J., and A.J. blamed his boss for not paying him on rain days. My skin blamed me for not putting myself up for adoption. I don't blame it one bit.

Whatever relationships you have attracted in your life at this moment, are precisely the ones you need in your life at this moment.[18]

—Deepak Chopra

---

[18] Lucky me.

Lily

Sunday, September 9, 2012

Blake wanted to go to the mall today but I couldn't. He really wanted an excuse to visit Mike, so I don't feel guilty. Mike is the crazy-jealous guy Blake has been "hanging with" since July. He works at J.Crew and, with the help of his employee discount, dresses Blake like Amelia Earhart.

"It's all leather bomber jackets and scarves this fall," he claims.

I want to say, "Really, Mike? Get a J.Clue. Blake is a skater, not a Tuskegee Airman!" But I don't. I once referred to him as Trike because he's a third wheel. Blake went radio silent on me for an entire day. I'm glad Trike doesn't live in our district or he'd be at Noble. And I'd become Lily, party of one.

Anyway, Mom and Dad wanted to go to ground zero to see the 9/11 memorial pools so we did that. I started crying when I saw the names of all the people who died. Which is weird because I was only five when it happened and I didn't know any of them. Maybe I was born with the unique ability to love people I've never met. This would explain my deep feelings for Duffy.

Epiphany! This trait must run in our family. Aunt Iris has an entire basement full of Elvis memorabilia and she's never met him either. She must have the same gene as I do. The one that makes me collect things Duffy has touched.

This is what I have so far:

- Crushed Mountain Dew can.
- Glow-in-the-dark Frisbee.
- Mud-covered Nike Air Max basketball shoes with the swooshes covered in silver duct tape.
- Reusable water bottle (blue).
- 3 used sparklers.
- Nerf water pistol.
- Purple-stained Popsicle stick.
- Basketball.

Lily Bader-Huffman-Duffy

Sheridan

9.10.12

INT. BATHROOM STALL—LAST PERIOD.

SHERIDAN had a choice to make: yawn through the last fifteen minutes of Algebra or put quill to paper and record her feelings while they were still raw. And ehmagawd, if you could smell what she's smelling, you'd know what she chose. SHERIDAN inhales the expired Chanel No. 19 on her wrist and begins...

Today started off ah-mazing.

FLASHBACK.

Audri got in the back of the BMW, took one look at me, and gasped. I was wearing a purple scarf side-tied around my neck, yellow cami, Max's gray church blazer, a pleated skirt, argyle knee socks, and sling-back wedges. My hair was reflective; my lips, glossed & found. She could not take her four eyes off me.

Um, Audri, are you an escalator? (Me.)

No, why?

Because you keep stair-ing. Now rate me.

Nine point five.

Why not a ten?

Because tens are reserved for special occasions!

Ahhhhhhhh! (That was both of us screaming at the same time because she was so right there with me on the *Clique* stuff.)

Ehmagawd, you're channeling Massie Block! (Audri.)

Dad turned up the volume on CNN Radio.

I think Isaac is getting annoyed. (Me.)

Audri cracked up so hard her entire face turned my favorite color. Hint: the color of royalty. Hint: Massie Block's favorite color. Anyway, Isaac was the Blocks' driver before (SPOILER ALERT) they went broke and had to fire him. Which, o'course, Audri knew because we were ob-suh-essed with that series in middle school.

I gave Audri a huge hug for naming my character so quickly. She pulled away fast.

Ew, what is that? (Audri fanning the air, ah-gain!) *Did you burp hand sanitizer?*

Puh-lease. (Me.) *It's Chanel No. 19. I found a sample in my mom's makeup cabinet. It's older than the feather hair-extension trend, but Massie wore it so . . .*

When Isaac dropped us at the Pick and Flick, I hooked my arm through Audri's and summoned "Don't Cha (Wish Your Girlfriend Was Hot Like Me)" on my inner iPod. Chins up, lips pursed, eyes knowing, we catwalked toward the school's arched entrance.

Everyone stared. I glared.

Duffy, the heart-drawing guy, side-eyed me again in English. So I thought:

Um, Sheridan, are you a hammer?

No, why?

'Cause you're nailing it!

I looked Duffy straight on and said, *Hey.*

His buddy Owen Cooper flicked him on the shoulder and they started laughing. I wanted someone to laugh with too. Instead, I rolled my eyes like they were so immature.

Attention up here, Miss Spencer, said Ms. Silver.

My blush blushed.

Science was next and I was determined to find a lab partner worthy of a place in my Pretty Committee.

I zeroed in on the girl with wavy hair and green eyes. She could be the exotic one, like Alicia. Together, we'd find a financially challenged athlete to play Kristen, and Audri would play Dylan. She wasn't big-boned or a redhead, but she thought burps were funny and was probably ready for a change after a three-year run as my Beta.

"Alicia" was so into taking notes she didn't notice me watching her. Thank Gawd! I didn't want to look desperate. But the second Mr. Larsen told us to choose a partner I pounced.

Her name was Vanessa. Which is kind of funny because she looks like Vanessa Williams from that show *Ugly Betty*, only younger.

Anyway, the assignment was to pick three substances and determine their effect on the boiling point of water. I asked Vanessa why this matters when we have microwaves. She didn't even smile. All she said was: *I'll choose the substances, work the Bunsen burner, and record our findings. You hold the beakers so they don't tip.*

Um, Vanessa, are you a designer named Hugo?

No.

Then why so Bossy?

Vanessa scratched her arms and then sat on her hands. *Sorry. What did you have in mind? You know, other than a microwave?*

I want to Bunsen.

Vanessa scratched again when Mr. Larsen came over and told us how well we were collaborating. So Vanessa, being the type who cares if science teachers like her, let it go.

First I lit the salt.

Then the sugar.

Then my scarf.

I screamed. Everyone screamed. Mr. Larsen blasted me with a fire extinguisher. Vanessa asked if she could start over with a different partner. I smelled like burnt stuffed animal. I looked like a marshmallow. That's what you get for wearing expired perfume.

It took most of Spanish to clean myself up and then it was lunch. I pulled Audri's secret note out from under the salad bar and squeezed it like a first Oscar.

It was all about the conversation she had with Jagger during lunch. I think she wants to lip-kiss him. Anyway, she went on and on about how he's being followed by a seal (whatever that means). Everyone at the table asked, what if this seal shows up at school? (What's the deal with this guy and animals?) Anyway, I started to panic. Did she really write "Everyone at the table"? EVERYONE? How many friends has Audri made? Two? Five? Seven? More than ten?

I lost my appetite (unusual for a "pear," I know) and have been light-headed and heavyhearted ever since.

Which brings me to now: last period, Algebra. And the part that's even more embarrassing than being publicly extinguished.

FLASHBACK. TEN MINUTES AGO.

I was in class, peeling off my purple nail polish, when the door opened.

Enter: California blonde; cut-off jean shorts, navy PUMA warm-up jacket, and knee-high glitter Converse.

Hello, Kristen! (Massie thinking that.)

Have a seat beside Sheridan. (Mr. Baskin.)

A few guys (and even some girls) turned to watch this tanned latecomer crop-dust our row with citrus-scented perfume.

They wanted in. I had to act fast.

What would Massie do? Smile? No, too wimpy. Pass a note? Too middle school. Impress her with a comeback? Ehmagawd, yes.

Are you pregnant? (Me, whisper-asking.)

She put a hand on her flat tummy and shook her head no.

So why did you miss so many periods?

Her lips curled into a grin. She leaned closer. *Are you a violent toddler?*

I giggled with anticipation. *No.*

Then why are you throwing Blocks?

Huh? Was she playing along or calling me out?

Silly Sheridan, cliques are for kids.

Mr. Baskin asked if he was interrupting her conversation. She said *no.* And then: *This girl beside me thinks she's Massie Block and I told her she should try to be herself instead. Or at least pick someone more current to copy.*

Everyone laughed. I grabbed my books and bolted for the bathroom. The bell just rang. I'm still here. I'm going to text Audri and tell her to go home without me.

Um, Sheridan, are you Green Giant Niblets?
No.
Then why do you live in the can?

To Be Continued...
END SCENE.

71

Jagger

Sept. 10.

I didn't get a lock.

Who's going to steal a bike from a kid with no parents?

Besides, I scraped the red paint off so it couldn't be ID'd. The reflectors are in the trash bin behind the pet store.

I tagged the seat with the price gun.

It wouldn't get a dime on Craigslist but the owner will never recognize it so I was relieved.

Until I saw the girl with blue glasses eyeing it after school. Was it hers?

— You into bikes or something?

She jumped back like I scared her. Then she giggled.

— Not really.

— We were at the same table for lunch today, right?

She nodded.

— I'm Audri.

— Jagger.

— I know.

— Detention?

— No. I usually get a ride with my friend but she's got...issues. I saw this crappy bike and thought it had been abandoned so...

— So you were going to swipe it?

She blushed.

— Too late, I already did.

I'm not sure why I told her that but something about her face made me feel safe.

— Want me to double you?

— Sure.

I did. It was cool. Audri's cool.

Time to feed the animals.

I wonder what she's doing right now.

-J

Sheridan

9.11.12

INT. SAME SMELLY PLACE AS YESTERDAY.

SHERIDAN's hair falls in soft waves. Dressed in a white skirt and matching warm-up jacket, she channels a person of great strength, determination, and blondness. A hardened athlete who is also super pretty. Tennis pro Anna Kournikova.

FLASHBACK TO EARLIER THAT DAY. EXT. NOBLE HIGH.

We had fourteen minutes before first period so Audri and I hung on the lawn and waited for my nemesis—aka the Algebrat. (Algebra + Brat = Algebrat.)

What are you going to say when we see her? (Audri.)

Nothing. I just want to show you who we're up against. Once you have a visual we can plot her demise.

TEN MINUTES LATER.

Is it possible you imagined her? (Audri.)

Maybe she transferred. (Me, hoping.)

What if she came from the spirit world? (Audri.)

Like one of those Shakespeare ghosts with a message? (Me.)

Or a warning. (Audri.)

Too far.

We were about to give up and head to class when a pink golf cart blasting "Party Rock Anthem" skidded to a stop at the Pick and Flick. Some guys started clapping. The girls squealed with fake embarrassment. I hated them already.

All short shorts and well-defined legs, the driver pinch-opened her hair claw and freed her own Anna K—type blondness while the trio headed down the path. When they got closer I realized it was her...she...whatever...the Algebrat!

I smacked Audri on the arm.

Where? (Audri.)

(Me, ventriloquisting.) *White tennis skirt, red warm-up jacket, glitter Converse. She's channeling me channeling Anna Kournikova!*

Except she appears to be a celery and you're a pear.

Uh, Без перевода. (Me, channeling Anna K.)

What? (Audri.)

That means "uh, thanks" in Russian.

Instead of laughing or maybe even apologizing, Audri lifted her blue glasses and squinted. *Octavia?*

Owdee? (Algebrat to Audri, only she called her Audi like the car.)

The first bell rang.

Octavia dropped her pink-and-silver Big Cat PUMA bag in the middle of the walkway and raced over to hug MY best friend.

O, that was the bell. (Her friend with the black ponytail.)

Octavia didn't answer because she was STILL hugging my best friend.

O! (Her friend with the brown ponytail.)

Meet ya.

The girls hurried off, sporty ponytails wagging goodbye.

Owdee, what are you doing at Noble?

I go here. (Audri.)

Lies!

Audri giggled. *Truths.*

You? Go to. My? School?

I stepped closer, reminding them I went there too.

Since when is Noble your school? (Audri sounding like an alpha.)

It's all mine, you know that.

They started cracking up like crazy.

After their over-the-top bout of hysteria, Audri finally acknowledged my presence and said, *You should see O play doubles. She calls "mine" on every ball. Even when it's on her partner's side. It's seriously the funniest thing ever.*

That's against the rules! (Me as Anna K.)

You know the rules? (Audri to me.)

I pointed at my Adidas logo and flashed extreme wide-eyes to remind her who I was channeling.

Oh yeah, sorry.

That's when Octavia looked at me kind of surprised, like I just showed up, and said, *Oh. Hey. I know you.*

Yeah, we kinda met yesterday. I folded my arms across my chest so she couldn't hear my heart.

You're the new locker room attendant at my racket club.

Audri giggled.

No, we have last period Algebra together.

We do?

I wanted to kick her bony undercarriage but I asked how they knew each other instead.

Camp Wildwood, they answered at the exact same time.

Only we didn't meet until the second-to-last day. (O.)

When we played each other in the Wildwood Wimbledon. (A.)

Which is such a boo-hoo because we would have been great partners. (O.)

Like I would ever be your partner. (A.)

Why? (O.)

Mine. Mine. Mine. (A.)

They cracked up again. (Barf. Barf. Barf.)

Lies! I wouldn't do that with you.

Lies! You would.

Wouldn't!

Would.

Would not.

Would yot.

Not.

Yot.

Yot? (O.)

Yot. (A.)

Laughter.

Audri, when did you get into court sports? (Me.)

I took a tennis clinic this summer. It's fun.

Fun?

Who are you, again? (Octavia.)

I'm Sheridan. Audri's best friend.

Best friend? (O.)

Audri put her arm around me. I grinned proudly and reiterated, *BEST*.

Octavia stepped closer. *Wouldn't a BEST friend know she plays tennis?*

Her question was a glitter high-top to the gut. But I was Anna K. It was my job to return the ball, not drop it. So I got all up in her tanned citrus-scented face and said, *Wouldn't a tennis player know not to cross the line?*

What line?

Theee line.

The service line or the baseline?

Theeeeeeeeeee line.

I'm sorry, I have no idea what line you're talking about.

The bell rang.

78

Game over.

Come on, you guys! (Audri.) *We should get to class.*

Octavia got her Big Cat PUMA from the path and asked Audri if she had early lunch or late. Audri said early. O'course Octavia has early too. Turns out they have the entire morning together so off they ran, leaving me with Zero-Love.

I spent all morning living for Audri's cafeteria note but got an apology text instead. Turns out she spent lunch listening to music in O's golf cart. I'm spending mine like a depressed Niblet—crying in the can.

Serves me right for channeling a tennis player who's never won a professional singles title.

To Be Continued ...

END SCENE.

DUFFY

Tuesday

According to Hud and Coops, Mandy looks like Kate Hudson and the guys at Noble think she's hot. Even though she's a junior and I'm just a freshman I feel like I have to protect her so I tell them to stop talking about her like a regular girl, but that makes them do it more.

Feeling = Disgusted.

They think her friends are pretty too. I've known them for like ever so I don't get all shy around them like Hud and Coops do, even though their hair smells like Hawaiian Punch and that's my favorite juice. Sometimes, when they say the space between my teeth is sexy my face goes red. When that happens

I look down at my sneakers and try to name the players on the Knicks.

Carmelo Anthony

Earl Barron

Tyson Chandler

...like that.

Junior guys are the worst. Especially when they don't know Mandy's my sister. They don't get why she's with a freshman and not them. Sometimes I put my hand on her shoulder. This messes them up even more.

Like today at lunch. She stops by my table to say she's working an extra shift at Abercrombie so I need to find my own way home. Right when she's telling me this some sophomore comes over and totally interrupts.

HIM: These boys giving you trouble?

Coops sneezed "Nehyyyy" because the guy had on one of those preppy polo shirts with the giant, steroided-out horse logo.

Hud laughed. I choked on a curly fry.

Then he started giving her a shoulder massage and telling her how tense she was and how she needed to relax. Hud and Coops looked at me like, are you okay with this? I wasn't but I wasn't okay with getting my ass kicked before tryouts either.

Mandy wiggled him off like a spider and said: Stop it Lo-gan!

Then Coops whispered: *Stop it Lo-go!*

We died at that.

Then Mandy's friend Morgan called him "sophomore" the

way Bubbie Libby calls our nameless dogs "animals" and Megan said: Pervert.

"Logo" put his hand on his heart/horse like he was all hurt and stuff, and said: Why d'ya have to take it there? I was just trying to be nice.

ME: Nice would be you leaving us alone.

The girls laughed—good for my ego, bad for my hoodie. Logo grabbed a handful of my fries, squeezed them between his sausage-fingers, and then smeared the potato guts on my back.

Feeling = Slick guys are the worst.

<u>Three things I'll never do:</u>

1. Talk like a cop and say, "These boys giving you trouble?"
2. Tell a girl she looks tense.
3. Name a kid Logan.

I'd never dress like some doof in a magazine ad either. Gardner's always getting some deal on designer brands but I wouldn't take that stuff for free. High-tops are the only exception and that's only because they don't come in plain. I wish they did because someone stole my lucky Nike Air Maxes and Mom said they're too expensive to buy again. It's all because of that swoosh. It jacks up the price. I bet they'd cost twenty bucks without it. Anyway, I cover my swooshes with duct tape.

Feeling = I don't do labels. I don't endorse for free.

Anyway, I wasn't about to let Logo get away with perving on Mandy and smearing on me. The guy had to be Wiped.

I did my first Wipe when I was eleven. Amelia wrote a play

called *Roll with the Punches*, about a girl named Jabby who falls down the stairs, ends up in a wheelchair, and becomes the best boxer in the world. Guess who played young Jabby?

Amelia made me practice falling every day after school until I got it right. It was awesome. We still lose it when we remember the time I did it for my parents. They came home from the real estate office with pizza and all these fountain sodas. The minute they opened the door I went rolling. We tied toy trucks to my shoelaces so it would sound really loud and clanky. Like teeth and bones.

I landed on my back and started twitching. Amelia and Mandy were cracking up. Mom started to cry. I was grounded for a month. It was worth it, though. Now I can fall like a stuntman.

Feeling = Logo is going down after school.

He takes the back stairwell, which was perfect. Fewer people meant fewer witnesses in case he decided to punch me or something. Hud and Coops were starting to laugh so I had to move fast. I snuck up behind Logo, and as soon as he cleared the first flight I turned to my side.

I put out my hands to lessen the impact. Then I ducked and rolled. I made my legs go all wild so everyone thought my body was out of control. Then I screamed: *Whoa!!!!!!* It's hard to describe the actual falling part because it happened so fast and I was spinning. But my landing was great. I bashed right into the back of Logo's legs and knocked him and his energy drink to the ground. Hud and Coops were losing it. I had to curl up in fetal and hide my face inside my hoodie so he wouldn't catch me laughing.

LOGO: What the hell, dude?

ME: Sorry, man, you okay? I totally tripped.

His buddies stood there while he looked down at his giant wet Polo pony. Pink drops dripped off his chin. It was so epic. Until he made a fist and pulled back his arm.

RANDOM GIRL: Stop!

Everyone turned around. It was my neighbor. The one that's always skateboarding by my house with her boyfriend.

SKATER GIRL: You okay?

I wanted to tell her it was all a joke and I wasn't hurt but then Logo would have punched me so I didn't.

ME: My ankle is a little sore but—

LOGO: What about me?

SKATER GIRL: You're fine.

LOGO: I'm not. There's a crack in my butt. Wanna see?

His friends high-fived. She kicked his backpack down the steps.

SKATER GIRL: Can you stand?

ME: I'll try.

Hud and Coops would have been all over helping her help me if she looked like Mandy, Megan, or Morgan (the 3Ms). But she's normal looking. Brown hair, brown eyes, saggy jeans, and yellow highlighter on her nails. Not bad. Just not slick. So they stood there.

LOGO: Hey, Freshman, I ever see you using these stairs again I'll hog-tie you to the back of my car and—

ME: Your lip is bleeding.

LOGO: Yeah? Well, next time it'll be your internal organs.

He drew back his fist again. I flinched and that made him happy. So he bolted.

I wanted to be alone with Hud and Coops so we could laugh about everything but Skater Girl was there and she was still trying to help me. So I kept wobbling and saying ouch and stuff like that. Hud and Coops couldn't stop laughing.

SKATER GIRL: What's so funny? He's hurt! What if he can't play basketball this season?

ME: How do you know I play basketball?

SKATER GIRL: You do? I had no idea.

ME: You just said—

SKATER GIRL: You're wearing high-tops. I guessed.

ME: Cool.

I stood and thanked her but she didn't leave. She just stared at me, like those hotel bellmen in the movies who want a tip. So I pulled a dollar out of my pocket and gave it to her. She didn't laugh, though. She squeaked like a happy mouse and put it in her pocket.

Feeling = Maybe she's poor.

—LATER

Lily

I touched Andrew Duffy! Andrew Duffy touched me!

I'm so excited I can't even write! Andrew Duffy fell down the stairs!!!! It was incredible.

I—Lily Bader-Huffman—literally slid my hands under his arms and lifted him to safety.

If it had been just the two of us, I think he would have let himself cry. But his loser friends were laughing at him so he had to keep it all inside. Desperate to show gratitude without betraying his machismo, he reached into the pocket of his jeans and pulled out a dollar bill. His greens were fixed on my browns as he extended his hand toward me. I offered mine in return. Our movements were smooth and exacting, as if we were performing ballet underwater. He placed the crumpled single in my open palm. A tip!

This must be a Pub thing. I was expecting something more traditional—more Homie—like verbal gratitude or a lingering handshake. But the dollar was way better. It gave us an excuse to touch. And now I can hold it. Treasure it. Ask it how it feels to spend an entire day pressed against his right leg.

I skated home so fast Blake thought I had to pee. I couldn't help it. I didn't want to hear about his day. I wanted to relive mine. Which I have, thousands of times. I even memorized the serial number on the bill.

L 89751377 D.

Can you believe those letters?? LD!!! L(ily) 89751377 D(uffy).

I love Pub!!!!

Lily Bader-Huffman-Duffy

Sheridan

INT. BEDROOM—NIGHT.

SHERIDAN is seriously depressed.

I waited until H&M were asleep and went looking for Mom. Not that she's an expert on O.L.S. (Overnight Loser Syndrome), but she's my mom. She has to love me no matter what. And I needed to feel loved.

I found her in the garage treadmilling on a full incline. I should have turned around then.

Any higher and you'll step on your ponytail. (Me.)

Gotta lose the baby (pant) *weight* (pant).

Mom, you had the twins seven years ago. Anyway, you're like a size zero.

Am (pant) *not. In certain jeans. I'm a* (pant) *two.*

Clearly she was the one suffering, you know, being an occasional size two and all. So I decided not to burden her with my O.L.S.—which, thanks to her, is now L.A.P.S. (Loser and Pear Syndrome). So I got snippy instead.

I just wanted to thank you for taking the little butt and giving me the big one. Your generosity has provided me with oodles of confidence.

Note: I have never used the word "oodles" before. Audri would have laughed.

Mom lowered the machine and slowed to a jog.

Sheridan, what's going on? Are you being teased about your weight? I think you look wonderful. But if you don't, we can put you on a program where—

Forget it! It's not about my weight, okay?

I stomped back to my room.

Even if I could have called CUT and SHERIDAN TALKS TO MOM ABOUT O.L.S.—TAKE TWO, I wouldn't have. I should have known better than to expect sympathy from a celery. Pears may have sturdy bases, but we are soft on the inside and should be handled with care. Walk the produce aisle and see for yourself. We're always bruised. But celeries? Ha! You need two hands to snap them.

PAUSE.

I just lit some sage. We used to burn it in the theater after plays to banish old characters and make way for new ones. I'm trying to banish Loser Sheridan so the popular one can return.

Loser Sheridan begone! (Me waving the plant over my bed.)

Popular Sheridan, beback! Loser Sheridan begone! Popular Sheri-
dan beback! Loser She—

Dad just came in and made me blow it out.

    Our house smells like the Occupy movement.

    Would you prefer the stench of loneliness?

    Please, Sheridan. Stop being so dramatic.

    Sure, Dad. And you stop being such a BMW dealer.

    S'cuse me?

    Nothing.

    I hate everyone.

To Be Continued...

    END SCENE.

Vanessa

September 12th

Forgive me, Journal, for I have sinned. It has been three days since my last entry.

Why, you ask? There is a shedload more homework in high school than in middle. And it's a little tiny bit hard.

Not that I can't handle it. I can. I totally can. I will! Last night, while savoring arrowroot biscuits and vanilla decaf, I reconsidered my social goals for the semester and concluded the following: Friends can wait. There's no one of any real interest anyway.

I was pursued by Sheridan Spencer in Monday's lab. But she was shallow and extremely flammable so I shut it down.

Ver? There is one girl I've been tracking. Not as a friend,

though. Strictly foe. Her name is Lily Bader-Huffman. We have English, AP World History, Algebra, and Global Media together. The girl ranks high on intel. She answers every question and knows things we haven't even been taught yet. I never even see her taking notes.[19] The point is, I suspect Lily Bader-Huffman may have the *60 Minutes* skill—and a few others, based on our lunchtime encounter.

Knowing that the list of awards, honors, and extracurriculars will be posted tonight,[20] I was determined to spend the first half of the week taking SWAP orders.[21] Because once that list goes up I'm going into O.M.[22] and my charity work will suffer as a result.

So, I was going table to table in the cafeteria, selling my last pieces of inventory. When a viselike force gripped the sides of my head and turned me toward a molten-hot guy. He waved me over. The moisture drained from my mouth.

He was sitting alone but didn't seem self-conscious about it.

....

[19] *60 Minutes* did a story about people who could remember every single detail from their past. The host would name a random date from twenty years ago and they would tell him exactly what they wore, ate, and did that day. At first, I thought it was the most enviable thing imaginable. Then I realized if I had it I'd remember every fight my family ever had. And that would make me itch more than I already do.

[20] Living for it.

[21] As of 1:14 PM today I am sold out of SWAP bracelets. Haiti is going to be so excited.

[22] Overachieving mode.

Why? Because tanned guys with careless dark hair and fudge-brown eyes only sit alone for one reason.[23]

"What are you selling?" he asked.

"SWAP bracelets," I answered.

I placed the prototype beside his orange tray and explained the concept. Which was not easy with him looking right at me. Usually boys get nervous around me. But this one crackled confidence.[24]

He nodded as if impressed and then offered me a warm hand in exchange for my name.

"Vanessa."

He snickered.

"What's so funny?"

"I wanted to try on the SWAP but it is really nice to meet you, Vanessa. I'm Blake."

My face turned the color of his pomegranate juice.

He took the bracelet from the table and fastened it around his wrist.

I never imagined it on a boy but I never imagined a boy who looked like Blake.

"That looks really good on you," I said, meaning it. The brown leather and gold envelope popped against his butterscotch-colored skin.

....

[23] They want to.

[24] Love that phrase. Ugh. Why isn't this journal being graded?

"Can I order two?"

My heart didn't skip a beat. It added one hundred more per second.

"Sure!"

He went on about how much he admired my passion and believed in my cause. He said it was refreshing to meet a pretty girl who cared about more than her looks. I turned pomegranate again.

He said it was cute when I blushed.

"What else are you into?" he asked. "Besides saving orphans?"

I wanted him to stop looking at me like that. I never wanted him to stop.

I had to sit. I would never ever eat in front of him, but my knees felt like they were being erased and I didn't want to fall.

I leaned on a chair for balance. I was about to sit when guess who arrived with tofu salad and two forks? That's right, Lily Bader-Huffman.

Foe no you diɀn't!

She was wearing pajama bottoms, and her gnawed fingernails had been jaundiced by a yellow highlighter. I needed to scratch. I balled my fists instead.

Was she pretty? Hmmm. Maybe in a "Before" picture kind of way. Bland, frizzy, unkempt, but symmetrical.

Still, no amount of symmetry could explain what Blake saw in her. Maybe they were cousins.

I had to get out of there before I whipped a piece of tofu at that talk-blocker's throat. Blake obviously got the second

SWAP for her and I did not want to be around when he fastened it to her bony "Before" wrist.

I can hear it now:

BLAKE: *Lily, just because you sold your soul to the devil in exchange for a* 60 Minutes *brain and an out-of-your-league boyfriend like me doesn't mean you're not worthy of a SWAP. So I bought you one. Correction: I bought us one. Poor Vanessa thought I bought two because I was flirting. Tragic, isn't it?*

LILY: *So what if the world sees me as a "Before" picture? You make me feel like an "After." A happily ever after...*

GROSS!

Now I'm in the study lounge, journaling about my first loss.

An overachiever could get used to this room. It's peaceful, grounding, and the couches are velvety soft. The vast collection of first edition novels invigorates my soul, the dim lights soothe it.

Jagger, the orphan, is seated across from me. He's writing and laughing to himself. Might he be a tad insane?

Ew. His dirty sneakers are on the cushions. Poor guy doesn't have anyone to teach him that shoes belong on the floor and not the furniture.

He's so thin.

He's closing his eyes. He must be exhausted from wandering the streets. Why doesn't the government do something for him? If I wasn't already committed to the Haitian orphans, I'd mentor him. But . . . Ver? It would do nothing for my GPA.

> *To acquire true self power you have to feel beneath no one, be immune to criticism and be fearless.*
>
> —Deepak Chopra

Jagger

I was hoping to see Audri at lunch but she wasn't there. Second day in a row.

Did I freak her out when we doubled home?

Something about her face (Blue glasses? Uneven smile? Freckle below her right eye?) said, "Go on, Jagger, tell me everything. Trust me with the extended-play version of your story. Life hasn't always been fair to me, either. I won't run. I won't ever run."

Still. I should have known better.

I should have left out the part about being followed by Pat, the ex–navy SEAL with a history of violence and a score to settle.

At least until she got to know me better.

But she seemed so interested and it felt good to talk.

Too many people know my deal.

Bags of clothes appear by my locker. I never eat lunch alone. Even the 3Ms say hi to me in the halls. But Pat knows too. I can feel it.

Bushes shake when I walk by. Camouflage blurs whip through my line of vision when I'm in crowded places. Randy's pets bang on their cages the moment I fall asleep.

Last time I visited Carla and Ed in prison they begged me to keep to myself. They made me promise.

Pat wants revenge. Payback for teaching Pat Jr. that lesson about bullying. And the best way to hurt my parents is to hurt me.

I should have kept my promise.

I really really should have kept my promise.

I should have kissed Audri instead of blabbing.

That kiss-butt Vanessa just sat on the couch across from me. She's journaling too. She keeps looking at me. She's scratching her arm like crazy, which makes me think she has some sort of communicable skin disease.

Contracting a communicable skin disease is no way to win Audri back.

Man, she's itchy.

Imagine if she lifted up her leg and started scratching behind her ear like Noodle did when he had fleas.

I just laughed out loud a little.

Uh-oh. She just smiled at me.

What if she wants to come over and talk? What if she asks me to join her on her infested communicable couch?

I can't let her think I am open to that.

Better fake sleep.

-J

DUFFY

Feeling = Someone does not want me to make Varsity.

Ever since Rosie the cleaning woman left, my lucky things have been missing. First my Nike Air Max shoes, then my basketball, now my red-and-white-striped sweatbands.

I searched the entire house and I still couldn't find anything. Probably because it's a mess in there. Mom keeps saying she's going to "tidy up" but she hasn't had time. Which is why I don't understand why they got rid of Rosie. Unless they caught her stealing my stuff. But why would Rosie take my sweatbands? She pinched her nose when I wore them.

———

Found them! They were in the laundry room about to get washed. Rosie never would have done that. She knew they held two years of victory sweat. Soap would destroy their powers. Without my Air Maxes and ball they are all the luck I have. I was so happy to have them back I actually hugged them. They smelled like Funyuns and winning.

Feeling = Back in the game.

I called Mom and made her swear she'd never ever, ever wash them. I was expecting her usual speech about making my own luck and how superstitions are for people who don't believe in themselves.

All she said was: Sounds good, Andrew.

Then she hung up.

Now I am in the rain, hiding behind the porch swing waiting for Coops to pick me up. Coops is always late. I'd rather be inside, but Bubbie Libby was cursing the coach for making basketball tryouts at 6 PM on a Friday because I will be gone for Sabbath dinner. I tried telling her it was the only time the gym was free but she wanted to write him a letter anyway. When she asked for the coach's name I said my ride was here and bolted.

It's kind of hard to journal in a crouched position but Ms. Silver said writing calms the nerves so I'm trying it. Not that I don't think I'll make the team. I'll make Freshman for sure. But I really want Varsity. Then I can travel and

I'm back. Ran drills. Did shooting lines. Suicides. Apes. Coach Bammer liked me because I didn't block out. I didn't ball hog, either. Coops said I had game face without looking too intense. This is good. Now I wait. I hate waiting.

Feeling = LeBron never has to wait.

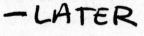

Lily

Saturday, September 15, 2012

The Homies (Blake, Hamilton, Legend, Wendi, Maple, Sylvie, and me) had plans to see *My Afternoons with Margueritte* at the Independent. I had to cancel because my Brit Lit essay is due on Monday and I'm only two paragraphs in. Not because it's hard. Nothing about Noble is hard. Mom used the ninth-grade curriculum guide when I was in seventh, so I've been coasting. It's my Mac that can't keep up.

I hit "save" after every sentence because my hard drive is old and forgetful. But every time I hit "save" I get the spinning wheel. Then it freezes. That's how I'm able to journal and write a paper on *Great Expectations* at the same time. I write during reboots.

Reboot successful.

Back to the essay.

~~~~~~

Rebooting again.

I have been saving for a new laptop since 2008. I got $1,018.00 for my bat mitzvah. My parents made me donate half of that to charity ($509) and put another $250 into Israel Bonds. This left me with $259. If you take inflation into account it's more like $237.62. Recycling cans at the grocery store would have been more lucrative.

I earn $25 for every A+ (again, cans would be easier) and only have to donate $5 of that to charity, which helps. Now, two years later, I am $150 away from a new computer.

My parents can afford to buy me one but they think saving will teach me the value of a dollar. This makes no sense. International markets, inflation, fiscal and monetary policy, fixed rates, floating rates, political instability, fluctuating demand, surpluses, and deficits determine the value of the dollar. Not my ability to save for a MacBook Pro.

Back to the essay.

~~~~~~

Rebooting again.

I met the Homies through a national organization that introduces homeschooled kids so we can have friends too. Ironically,

I had more of a social life when I was stuck at home. Must research ways to fit in. Noble has been kind of tough in that area. I'll do that after I finish my essay.

I haven't seen the Homies since I went Pub. Which is tragic because we were tight. Blake, Hamilton, Legend, Wendi, Maple, Sylvie, and I used to meet for gelato every Wednesday. Even in the winter. We took music, soccer, and art classes at the community center. We had (supervised) coed sleepovers and giggled about our CNN anchor crushes. Legend's dad, Maverick Lustig—yes, THE Maverick Lustig, four-time X Games champion, pro rider, spokesmodel, and owner of Lord's Boards—taught us to skateboard. That's like having Stephen Hawking as a science teacher.

When Blake heard I couldn't go to the movie today, he bailed too. He said he had a migraine, but GPS tells a different story. According to Find My Friends, he's at the mall. Probably meeting Trike on his lunch break. I bet Trike is pirouetting through the fountains because I'm not there. If he knew how many girls check Blake out at school, he'd flip his 40 percent off chambray trilby lid. Especially if he saw the way Vanessa looked at Blake in the cafeteria the other day.

Why Trike would flip his 40 percent off chambray trilby lid is the part I don't get.

As females, we pose no threat whatsoever. Blake says Trike is possessive because his father walked out on him when he was four, leaving him with a bitter mother and heinous abandonment issues. I'm not heartless. I understand how that would mess a guy up. But jealous of girls?

Whenever I ask Blake why he puts up with Trike's possessiveness he starts to wheeze. He says I'll understand when I'm in love, and then changes the subject. I want to tell him I am in love and I still don't understand. But I'm not ready to tell him about Duffy. So I say, "You're probably right."

~~~~

Rebooting.

I haven't told Blake about Duffy because he, along with the other Homies and the entire Bader-Huffman clan, expects me to marry Seth Cohen from *The O.C.* Not Adam Brody, the actor who played Seth Cohen. The actual character. They think this because:

1) Seth Cohen is intellectual, quirky, neurotic, athletically challenged, kind, Jewish, and probably lactose intolerant. So am I.
2) I was madly in love with Seth Cohen from 2007–2010. I watched every DVD at Blake's house because we don't have a TV. I told my parents Seth Cohen was a junior senator so I could hang his picture in my room without getting a lecture on idol worshipping.
3) Blake said I was obSethed.

And then there's Andrew Duffy: the anti–Seth Cohen. He is an all-American athlete. Honey-blond hair. Green eyes. Minimally expressive. Angst-free. A typical male. The boy next door. Conventionally handsome. Quirk-less. Lactose tolerant. Normal.

As a Jewish Homie with a gay best friend, five worn-out skateboards, a passport stamp from twenty-two different countries, dial-up Internet, and a wardrobe that doubles as flu-wear, I am drawn to "normal" like Odysseus to Sirens. I am over having a life that only six people can relate to. Simply put: I don't want abnormal to be my normal anymore.

I want to go to dances and forbidden house parties. I want to cheer for my boyfriend from the bleachers. I want to hold his hand after the game. I want to have unintellectual, stilted, benign conversations. I want to stop using words like "benign." I want to share non-kosher snack foods with him. Snack foods that are full of preservatives and additives. I want to see formulaic horror films at a multiplex. Films that are called movies. Movies that are not remakes of a foreign version that was far superior. I want Duffy to kiss me on that patch of narrow grass between our houses. I want to build a wobbly wood plank and set it between our windows so we can sneak into each other's rooms after bedtime. I want to get caught and lectured. I want to shout about not being understood. I want to get grounded. I want Duffy and me to find ways to be together anyway. Most of all I want him to like me because he thinks I'm just like him.

Back to my paper.

Lily Bader-Huffman-Duffy

110

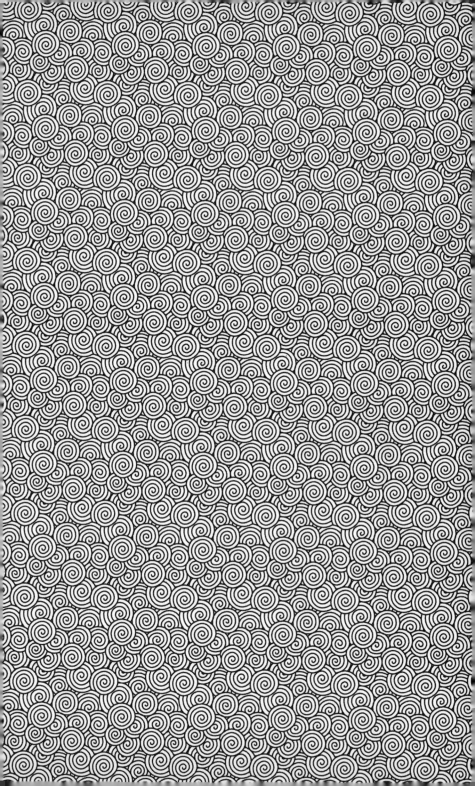

DUFFY

Feeling = I SERIOUSLY hate waiting.

I better make Varsity. I have to make Varsity. Twenty-two more hours until Monday, September 17th, and I'll know if I made Varsity.

If I can write Varsity forty times in under one minute I will make it. Ready, set, go!

Varsity vars

35.

Feeling = Crap.

VARSITY VARSITY
VARSITY VARSITY
VARSITY VARSITY
VARSITY VARSITY
VARSITY VARSITY
VARSITY VARSITY
VARSITY

Jagger

I saw Audri in American History this morning.

Her T-shirt was the same color blue as her glasses.

I asked if she bought them as a set.

Mr. Rosen told us to take our seats before she could answer.

I spent the entire period jamming a pen into my fingertip. I needed to feel something other than what I was really feeling which was: Jagger, why did you ask about her shirt when what you really wanted to say was, don't be afraid to hang out with me.

When class was over Audri said she did not buy her shirt and glasses as a set.

I thanked her for letting me know. Not because I care if matching things are sold separately or together. But because she remembered I asked. Because she pushed past other boys to catch up with me. Because she wasn't afraid.

I wanted to hug her.

I didn't.

She started to giggle.

I asked her why.

She said I was holding a FemFresh pen which was weird because I'm a guy and FemFresh is a tampon company.

I told her it came in the FemFresh case we got for our journals. I asked if she got one too.

She didn't.

I said I thought FemFresh was an organic food company.

She laughed.

I thanked her for letting me know and tossed the pen. It landed in an open locker.

We laughed.

A: What are you doing for lunch?

J: Eating.

I told her she could eat with me today if she wasn't afraid.

A: Afraid of what?

I was going to say Crazy Pat the ex–navy SEAL but why go there?

J: Afraid of me.

A: Why would I be afraid of you?

J: PMS.

She laughed. She got my reference to the FemFresh pen and laughed! She got *me*.

During lunch I told her how hard it is to visit my parents in jail.

Her eyes teared up.

Then she started crying.

I wish I hadn't told her any of that.

We are still at lunch. She's writing her friend Sheridan a note so I decided to write this. Something to do.

Beats staring.

Vanessa

September 17th

Forgive me, Journal, for I have sinned. It has been five days since my last entry.

Ver? I wasn't going to write today either. I was going to spend lunch reviewing my Algebra flash cards. When a Fem-Fresh pen literally flew into my locker. If that isn't a sign to journal[25] please tell me what is.

The honors and awards posting came out last week and it's full of opportunities. I'm going for:

....

[25] The journal came in a FemFresh case.

<u>Academic Excellence.</u> (GPA of 3.75 or higher)

<u>Honors Society.</u>

<u>Principal's Award.</u> (nominated by the cafeteria cooks, secretaries, and custodians)

<u>Track Team.</u> (I already made track team. I can't be captain until my senior year but Coach Speedman[26] said he will help me work toward that goal.)

<u>The Phoenix Five.</u> This opportunity only exists at our school but it's still really important. Last year's winners were contacted by college scouts. I took a picture of the flyer. This is what it said:

FRESHMEN ONLY

NOBLE HIGH'S *PHOENIX* YEARBOOK STAFF WANTS TO HONOR FIVE OF TOMORROW'S LEADERS, TODAY. NOMINEES MUST BE ABLE TO THRIVE UNDER PRESSURE, ADAPT TO NEW SITUATIONS, MAKE FRIENDS EASILY, STAND OUT IN A CROWD, SET TRENDS, AND ACHIEVE.

NOMINATIONS BEGIN IN APRIL.

VOTE FOR THE WINNERS IN MAY.

....

[26] No. I did not make that up. My track coach's last name is actually Speedman.

OUR FIVE MOST OUTSTANDING FRESHMEN WILL BE
NAMED IN THE 2012–2013 *PHOENIX* YEARBOOK.

MAKE YOUR MARK NOW. FIGHT FOR A PLACE AMONG THE
PHOENIX FIVE IF YOU PLAN TO PURSUE A CAREER AS A
POLITICIAN, CEO, NEWS ANCHOR, PERFORMER,
PROFESSIONAL ATHLETE, MOTIVATIONAL SPEAKER,
BESTSELLING AUTHOR, SPIRITUAL LEADER, OR
CELEBRITY CHEF.

WHO WILL BE THIS YEAR'S PHOENIX FIVE?

1. _____
2. _____
3. _____
4. _____
5. _____

I signed up for all five spots.

More later. Wish me luck on my Algebra quiz. I'm craving
Benihana.

Good luck is opportunity meeting preparedness.

—Deepak Chopra

Sheridan

9.17.12

INT. MASTER LO's TAE KWON DO STUDIO—LATE AFTERNOON.

SHERIDAN's O.L.S. has been lifted. Order has been restored.

Pass the mic, Ms. Justice, there's a new Victorious in town!

Mom's the one freaking out now. She's pacing Master Lo's waiting room because H&M are testing for their green belts. Her big fear? One will pass and the other will fail. In which case she'd rather they both fail. How weird is that?

I was going to call her on it but decided to put quill to paper instead. I'd rather focus on the positive. For instance, I went to school as Sheridan Spencer today and it wasn't a total disaster.

The freshman play was announced and I wanted to be me when I got the news. I didn't even wear a costume, just skinny jeans, orange ballet flats, a plain white tank top, and a navy cardigan. I pinned back a chunk of hair by my ear and dusted my cheekbones with pink blush. Audri said I looked pretty in a regular way.

She must have been right because that Zero Direction guy who blamed Audri for the rain on our first day of school came right up to me to talk about Dad's BMW M5. I thanked him and told him about the dealership. He said I was lucky because he's obsessed with cars and his dad has a boring job at a law firm. Then he asked if I have ever heard of the M3 GTR. I told him we have the 2013. He said You mean the one in Gran Turismo? I said yep. He said noooooo wayyyyyyyyy and then bowed like I was royalty. I felt special.

How do you know Logan? (Audri.)

I don't. How do you know Logan?

Octavia's dying to make out with him.

Too late.

Why?

He's in love with a model.

Who? (Audri, pushing her blue glasses up her nose.)

The 2013 M3 floor model.

We cracked up.

Anyway, the freshman play is *Wicked*. Last year I was Elphaba the bad witch and I dream of playing Glinda next. Everyone in drama club said I sound like Kristin Chenoweth when I sing

"Popular" so I'll audition with that for sure. O'course Audri will too.

Everyone thinks it's weird that she wants to be my understudy. Then we explain it's the only way Audri can play lead and they get it.

Audri is good. She has range, focus, and the unmatched ability to cry on demand. But I'm better. I'm not bragging. It's a fact. I work harder and am constantly studying the craft. So I always get lead. I knew this bothered Audri so I made her a secret deal. If she'd volunteer to be my understudy I would "act" sick at least one night (more if it's a long run) so she can have a turn in the spotlight. She cried for real when she heard the offer and said I was the best friend ever. I cried for real too because I was happy she was happy. So we've been doing it for the past two years.

Having played both leads will really round out our list of credits. We're going to start practicing tomorrow after school. Auditions are this Wednesday. I wanted to start tonight but Mom said I should be here for my brothers because green belt is a big deal. Oh, and Glinda's not?

Audri left me a lunch note today! She ate with Jagger. He told her about visiting his parents in jail. Aside from bully beating they are normal and shouldn't be behind bars. He knows the whole emancipation thing broke their hearts but what choice did he have? He couldn't exactly run to jail every time he needed a field trip permission slip or report card signed.

Audri wondered if she was heartless because she couldn't cry during Jagger's tragic story. All she could think about was kissing him. She ended up faking it. And the Oscar goes to Meryl Weep.

Normally hearing that Audri has a crush and wants to kiss would make me feel heavy. I'd wonder why I didn't have a crush or why kissing still scares me and not her. But I'm not wondering any of that right now. I'm too busy being happy she wasn't eating lunch with Octavia. Maybe they got in a fight.

Remember that guy Duffy? The one who was making hearts about me in English? Well, his locker is across from mine and today I heard him whistling. The song sounded familiar but I couldn't figure out what so I moved closer and listened harder. Then it hit me. It was "I Feel Pretty" from *West Side Story*. I was shocked.

Maybe, if I had to stretch my imagination, I could picture Andrew Duffy whistling "Jet Song" or "Cool." But "I Feel Pretty"? I had to ask.

I must have freaked him out because he jumped and slammed his locker.

Huh?

I said, Are you singing "I Feel Pretty"?

He turned red and kind of giggled. *Oh, I dunno. Was I? Maybe.*

Really?

Two sisters. He looked down the hall and then leaned closer like he was about to tell me a secret. He smelled girly, like baby powder deodorant. *They force-fed me show tunes when I was little. Sometimes I spring a leak and one dribbles out.*

I giggled. It was an odd choice of words for a basketball player. I could tell by the duct tape on his high-tops that he probably had other odd things to say.

So, do you feel pretty today?

He flipped up the hood of his sweatshirt and stuffed his hands in his pockets. *If you must know I changed the lyrics to I feel happy.*

Why?

Because I don't feel very pretty today.

No, I meant, why do you feel happy?

I made the Varsity team. So did my best friends.

Congratulations.

Thanks. You're in my English class, right?

I am.

You wore red lipstick on the first day of school.

I looked down at my orange ballet flats.

I remember that. (Duffy.)

Really? (Me. Voice shaking.)

Yeah.

Wow. Good memory.

Yeah, well, you smiled and—

And what? (I knew he had a crush on me! I couldn't wait to tell Audri.)

You had red shmeared all over your tooth. Like you got punched in the mouth.

Oh.

Normally I would have wanted to cry and die and then reincarnate, cry some more, and die again. But the space between his teeth made me feel like he didn't expect people to be perfect.

I'll make you a deal. (Me.)

What?

If you promise to tell me when I have lipstick on my teeth I'll tell you when you have pee spots on your jeans.

He laughed and then introduced himself. I did the same.

Nice to meet you, Sheridan.

This made me smile because it really was Sheridan he was meeting. And he liked her.

By the way. (Duffy, locking his locker.) *You don't need lipstick.*

And you don't need jeans. (Me, slapping my hand over my mouth.) *Oh my god, I didn't mean it like that. I don't even know what I meant.*

Yeah, right. (Duffy, walking away acting like he wasn't buying it.)

Uh-oh. Tae Kwon Do testing is over. Results coming in... and...

Both boys failed. Mom is relieved. A good day indeed.

To Be Continued...

END SCENE.

Lily

Monday, September 17, 2012

All of the "normal" social clubs were filled by the time I got to school today because normal people signed up online over the weekend. Whereas, I had to send smoke signals, which have yet to arrive.

Which brings me to another reason I want to be normal. Normal people have parents with cable modems. But my mom? She sees dial-up as a teaching tool. She says my generation's dependence on instant gratification will lead to our downfall and some things are worth waiting for.

"Why?" I argue.

"Because no one gets what they want the minute they want it."

"They do on the Internet," I tell her.

"Well, it's not realistic," she says.

"Actually, the Internet is very real."

"Don't be smart, Lily," my dad says.

"Then stop teaching me so much."

We always have arguments like these. The only one I ever won was when they let me go Pub. Unfortunately, I don't feel like much of a winner when I'm there so I'm not sure it counts.

There was one opening left—in the style club—so I went for that. I was told to come back when I get style. Blake laughed. I wanted to cry. But I didn't until I spotted this super-pretty blonde talking to Duffy at his locker today. Her name is Sheridan Spencer. She could have been CEO of the style club. Her whole "classic-cardi-meets-an-unexpected-pop-of-orange-ballet-flats" had me wondering if she spent the weekend playing dress-up with Trike.

Blake did, that's for sure. He showed up today all dapper in a faded gingham shirt, distressed jeans, and pop-of-red New Balance sneakers.

The style club girls literally applauded him in the halls.

During lunch (homemade kosher salami sandwich and a pickle) I said, "How can I possibly compete with Pub girls like Sheridan Spencer when I dress like a Homie with mononucleosis?" Naturally, Blake asked if I liked anyone. I said no but I might someday and I want to be ready.

"How much money do you have?" he asked.

"None."

"Don't you have nine hundred bucks?"

"Yeah, but that's for my laptop."

"Can you dip in?"

"No! I've been saving for two years."

"Hmmm. I have some old pj's that might fit you."

"Ew."

He took a bite of his cheeseburger. I tossed my thickly sliced salami in the trash and tried to swallow the mustard-covered rye. "If I get perfect on my Algebra quiz today, I'll get twenty-five bucks. Twenty after my charitable deduction."

"Maybe Mike can hook you up with his employee discount. You could get some jeans. Or maybe we should start with a shirt. Or shoes. Or a haircut." He looked at my drawstring pants and sighed. "You're the charity case. You should pocket the full twenty-five."

I whipped my mustard rye at his cheek even though Blake was right. I am a mess. So I spent the rest of the period cramming for my $25 Algebra quiz. I'll ace it. That class is so seventh grade.

Like my clothes.

Lily Bader-Huffman-Duffy

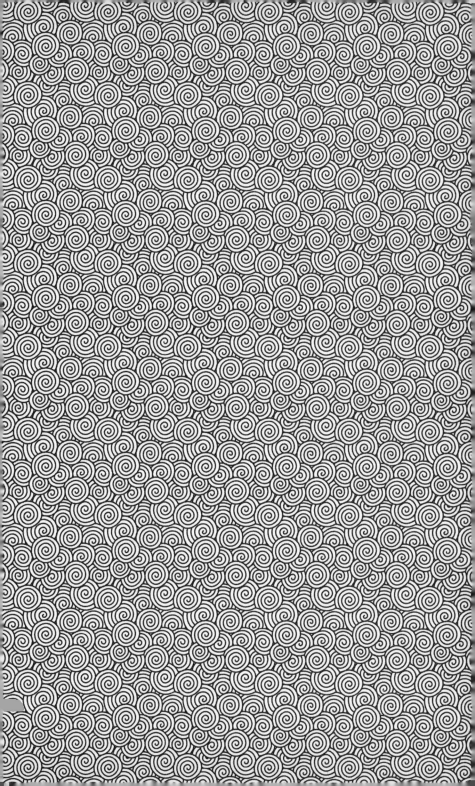

Vanessa

September 17th

Forgive me, Journal, for I have sinned. It has been less than a day since my last entry so that's obviously not it. It's something else. And it's worse than not journaling.[27]

As you know, I had an Algebra quiz today. You also know I studied during lunch so I was prepared. What you don't know is that the "Before" picture sat beside me in Algebra and completely disrupted my chi.

"You're too funny," she said.

"I am?"

---

[27] Way worse.

"I love how you signed up for every spot on the Phoenix Five. Hilarious."

"Why?"

"Why? Those blank spaces were rhetorical."

Foe no you diʒn't! This was her trying to rile me up before the quiz. It was a total power move. But she'll have to fight smarter than that if she wants to beat me to the Academic Excellence award, the Honors Society, and the Principal's Award. As for the Phoenix Five, she can have one spot if she really wants. I'll take four.

"I really like those bracelets you're selling."

"SWAPs."

"Sorry."

"I'm sure you'll be very happy with yours," I snipped.

"Mine? I didn't get one."

"You will."

"Huh?"

"Your boyfriend bought two."

"Boyfriend?" She looked confused and then kind of laughed. "You mean Blake?"

I stared at her again.

"He's not my boyfriend. He's—we've been best friends for years."

"I think he likes you."

"There is nothing between us. Trust me."

"Really?"

"Cross my heart." She made an X over her ill-fitting shirt. "Never has been. Never will be."

"Does he have a girlfriend?"

"Nope."

"Oh," I said, like I didn't really care. But on the inside my cells were popping like kernels in a microwave. Blake was single. He didn't like Lily![28]

I wanted more intel but Mr. Baskin started handing out the quiz. We had twenty minutes to answer ten questions.

I tried to focus but Blake's dark eyes waxed in my mind and eclipsed my math knowledge.[29]

Still, I finished first. Eighteen minutes and twenty-three seconds. Instead of taking our quizzes home and grading them like a responsible teacher, Mr. Baskin had us switch papers with the person sitting next to us. Lily got mine and I got hers. He called out the correct answers while we, the students, graded them. It was a total sweatshop move.

Lily got ten out of ten.

I got eight.[30]

When you make a choice, you change the future.

—Deepak Chopra

---

[28] Not that I care. I have to focus on my work. It's just nice to know he doesn't like *her*.

[29] Love the image of Blake's eyes as the moon eclipsing my rational thoughts. So poetic.

[30] I "accidentally" took Lily's paper so I could pass it off as my own. I needed a Benihana night. Don't judge.

Sheridan

9.19.12

INT. STARLIGHT AUDITORIUM—BACK ROW.

SHERIDAN as KRISTIN CHENOWETH, Tony and Emmy award winner, exits the stage after her first high school audition. She performed like a hammer and nailed it.

As planned, I sang "Popular" from *Wicked* in 32 bars. I began with the first verse after the intro ("Popular, you're gonna be popular" thru "everything that really counts to be..."), then cut to the last ("very very popular like me") and finished strong with "La la la la, you'll be popular, just not quite as popular as me!"

Coherent sense? Check.

Actable? Check, check.

Set me up for the last big belt note? Don't make me say it again.... Okay, fine... CHECK!

There, the facts have been documented. My memoirs will be accurate. In a perfect world I'd put quill to paper and record the other stuff that happened during the audition. But I'm way too emotional. And my world is light-years away from perfect.

To Be Continued...

END SCENE.

DUFFY

Friday

Bubbie Libby always says: Andrew, life is like a giant hemroyd (sp?); sometimes it's up, sometimes it's down.

ME: I hear ya.

I only said that because it's funny when she talks about hemroyds and I don't want her to stop. But I never actually got it until now.

It's night. I'm in a tent. Dad is snoring. I can't sleep. Not after what he told me. I'm watching the campfire, thinking about the hemroydian week I just had. Up one minute, down the next. Right now it's crazy-down.

Feeling = Good news if you're a hemroyd. Bad news if you're me.

It started with me, Hud, and Coops making Varsity. Coach Bammer said it's the first time ever that three freshmen made his team. Then he pulled me aside and said he'd be watching me. He thinks I have a very bright future in this sport if I want it.

ME: Of course I want it.

HIM: Then I'm going to push you.

ME: Cool.

That was up. The down happened when we were leaving the locker room. I was wondering what that girl Sheridan eats for breakfast when, out of nowhere, this arm grabs Hud's shirt and pulls him back in.

LOGO: How much did you pay?

HUD: For what?

LOGO: For your pedicure, what do you mean for what? For your spot on the team?

I yanked Hud away.

LOGO: Wrong answer.

He drew back his fist and aimed it at my face. Just as he was about to strike, Coops sideswiped Logo's fist with some brown-belt karate action.

COOPS: Keee-ai!

He landed like he was straddling a toilet.

COOPS: Prepare for epic battle.

Logo pushed Coops into a locker and grabbed Hud's uniform for the second time. He flicked the sponsor's name and said: explain *that*.

HUD: First Rate Real Estate?

LOGO: Isn't that your daddy's business?

HUD: So?

LOGO: So? You sweat freshman piss in basketball but for some straaaaange reason you're on the Flames and I got cut.

COOPS: He's better than you.

LOGO: Come here and say that.

Coops stepped right up to Logo but instead of saying: he's better than you, he shouted Keee-ai! and round-housed Logo in the shin. No one saw it coming. Not even me and I've known the guy since first grade. It was sick! Until Coops tried to run and wiped on the wet tiles.

He has to wear one of those black Darth Vader boots for seven weeks, maybe more. So he's out for the season. Logo got his spot.

That

was

a

down

day.

The rest of the week was about drills and schedules. Bammer said we'd be closer than brothers by the end of the year. I said cool because I'm sick of sisters. Everyone laughed. Logo cracked his knuckles.

Feeling = Over that guy.

Other than Logo, everyone seems cool. They know Hud and I have skills and keep saying how the Noble Flames are going to dominate this year. Greg, one of the seniors, even offered to drive me to practice and stuff so I don't have to deal with my parents. The way he said it made me think he has annoying parents. I like mine and normally I'm cool if they want to take me to games but Mom has been stressed lately so I said okay.

Like Wednesday after practice. I was in the kitchen swigging chocolate milk from the carton when she showed up. Carrying a laundry basket! Normally she freaks when I drink from the carton but she didn't even notice. All she cared about was my uniform which I guess she had just washed.

MOM: Hudson's parents are sponsoring the Flames?

ME: Yeah.

MOM: Since when?

ME: Dunno.

MOM: Does your father know?

ME: Dunno.

MOM: Well, what *do* you know?

ME: I dunno. What's the big deal?

MOM: The big deal is it costs money to sponsor a team.

ME: So.

MOM: So, I guess they're having a good year.

ME: Maybe you should get Rosie back.

MOM: Rosie? What does Rosie have to do with anything?

ME: You seem kinda...I dunno. Maybe you need help or something.

141

MOM: You're right.

So you know what she did? She handed me the basket and told me to put the clothes away. Then, after tripping over our nameless dogs and shouting the s-word, she went upstairs to take a bath.

I put the basket in Mandy's room with a note that said, **Mom wants you to put these away.** Then I played DS.

Feeling = If she wants to wear slick designer clothes she should put them away herself.

Today Coach Bammer sent us home with the parents' packet. We have to bring it back Monday with everything signed and paid for or we're off the team. Varsity is that serious. I gave it to Dad right when he got home. He was in my room ten minutes later.

ME: That was fast. Thanks.

He dropped it on my bed and asked if I wanted to go fly-fishing.

ME: When?

DAD: Now.

ME: It's Sabbath.

DAD: We're not Jewish.

ME: Oh yeah.

Feeling = Either my parents are dying or they're getting divorced.

Dad and I have been going on these awesome guys-only fly-fishing trips since I was six. With Varsity we probably won't have time for them so I brought my journal. I thought it would be good to take notes so I could remember the good times, just in case my last feeling comes true.

Feeling = It better not.

We listened to the Yankees game for most of the drive. They were down by three in the last inning. Dad turned it off.

ME: Why'd ya do that?

DAD: I'm tired of losing.

ME: I hear ya.

I had no clue what he was talking about.

We pulled off the highway and onto the dirt road that led to our campsite. Twigs snapped under the weight of our 4Runner. Rocks and roots were pressed into the mud. Tree branches scraped along our windows like witch nails. These were the only sounds we heard for the last few miles. I liked it that way.

We pulled into the campground and parked. Dad gripped the steering wheel and lowered his head. He seemed nervous. He wanted to tell me something but was afraid.

Feeling = He's dying.

I started naming Knicks to stay calm. Carmelo Anthony, Earl Barron, Tyson Chandler...

I got all the way to J.R. Smith before he looked at me.

DAD: Twenty-five hundred dollars?

ME: Huh?

DAD: Are you playing on a team or buying one?

ME: What are you talking about?

DAD: The fees. They're outrageous.

ME: I hear ya. It's the travel and motels and stuff. We're playing fifteen away games. Coach Bammer said it would be double that if First Rate wasn't sponsoring us.

DAD: Yeah, I heard about that.

He said it like it was bad news.

ME: Hey, maybe if Duffy Commercial Realty sponsored us too it would be cheaper.

Dad said "ha" but didn't laugh.

I started to freak.

ME: Do you have a disease?

DAD: No.

ME: Does Mom? *Bubbie?*

DAD: Why would you think that?

ME: You guys have been acting all weird lately.

He lowered his head on the wheel again. I was freaking so hard I grabbed his biceps. It used to feel stronger.

ME: You're scaring me, Dad. What is it?

DAD: Can I trust you?

ME: Yeah.

DAD: No, really.

ME: 'Course.

DAD: Son—

ME: What?

DAD: Your mother and I filed Chapter Eleven.

ME: Oh.

DAD: I know what you're thinking.

ME: You do?

DAD: You're wondering how we let it come to this. Believe me, I ask myself the same thing.

ME: No I'm not.

DAD: You're not?

ME: No. I'm thinking, what-in-the-H is Chapter Eleven?

For some reason this made him want to hug me.

DAD: Let's set up camp.

So we set up camp, started a fire, and cooked hot dogs. Then he explained.

DAD: Chapter Eleven means bankrupt. I can't pay the bills.

ME: What bills?

DAD: Mortgage, payroll, company cars, gas—

For some reason that orphan Jagger popped into my brain. Would people be leaving clothes by my locker soon, too?

ME: What about food?

DAD: No one is going to starve. Don't worry. But we did close Duffy Commercial. It was the only way to get out of the red.

ME: The red?

DAD: It's an expression. It means out of debt. We have to start a whole new business. We've laid the groundwork but it will take time.

He threw his hot dog into the fire. We watched it burn. I wondered if he should be wasting food.

He told me it was crucial that I not tell anyone about this. Especially Hudson. First Rate is their top competitor and he doesn't want them poaching Duffy's clients. The only way they will be able to make a quick recovery is if this stays a family secret. He made me promise to keep it. I did.

We got in the tent and zipped up our sleeping bags. Then he said one last thing.

DAD: Our family will have to make sacrifices, you know. A lot of them.

ME: Like eating Mom's cooking?

He laughed.

ME: Is that why we got rid of Rosie?

DAD: Yes.

He rolled over so his back was to me.

Coyotes yelped all around us.

DAD: That's why I can't pay your basketball expenses.

ME: What?

DAD: I'm sorry, son.

My legs went numb. My lungs turned to stone. I wasn't yawning but it was hard to hear.

ME: Can you lend me the money? I'll get a job and pay you back right away. A bit each week. I promise.

DAD: My funds have been frozen.

ME: But—

DAD: I'm sorry.

We didn't say anything after that. We just lay there, hands folded across our chests, staring up at the canvas roof.

Eventually Dad fell asleep. I am back outside. How am I going to get $2,500 by Monday?

I am throwing dry leaves into the fire.

Feeling = Jealous of dry leaves.

They get a chance to play with the Flames.

I never will.

Vanessa

September 22nd

Forgive me, Journal, for I have sinned. I should be asking for forgiveness, only Dad says when a person is forgiven they must never do that wrong thing again.[31] And I can't promise that. Because the wrong thing I did led to ~~good great~~ amazing things. So I'm not unequivocally sorry.

Cheating is for desperate losers and my brother. So, naturally I had second thoughts about passing "Before" Picture's A+ off as my own. Besides, I didn't get a B+ because I'm stupid. I got a B+ because BP told me that Blake was not, in any way,

---

[31] Referring to switching quizzes with the BP—"Before" Picture.

her boyfriend. Thusly, it triggered a serotonin surge in my frontal lobe.[32] Considering I was under the spell of powerful monoamine neurotransmitters,[33] I think I did well. Besides, it was only a quiz.

When I got home Mom was in the kitchen flipping through a cookbook. Dad crunched a credit card bill in his fist.

"Who spends four hundred and fifty dollars on shoes?"

"Boots," she said. "And I need them for work."

"Odette, you sit behind the concierge desk. No one is looking at your feet."

"Is that what you think I do? Sit behind a desk all day?"

I started to itch.

"Well, don't you?"

Mom shut the cookbook. "No, that's what *you* do. Only you're not interacting with humans. Just computers. Which explains your people skills."

"At least I *have* people skills."

"I was being facetious."

"Really? I thought you were being a b—"

"Hey," I called, paper-cutting the tension with Lily's A+. "Guess what I got?" I pressed my thumb over her name

---

[32] It's possible she did this to take me down and eliminate her competition. Must keep an eye on her. Friends close, enemies closer kind of thing.

[33] Wikipedia.

and flashed the olive branch. Then I stuffed it in my bag and welcomed their hugs. "Beni's tonight?"

Mom said, "I wasn't in the mood to cook anyway."

"Are you ever?" Dad hissed.

And that was that. We spent the rest of the night stealing shrimp off each other's plates and sharing the details of our day.

After Oskar brought out our Bindi orange sorbets and pineapple boat A.J. said, "This was so much fun. Let's do it again tomorrow."

I kicked him under the table because who gets A's on a Sunday? I resented the added pressure.

"Relax, Nessa. I've got it."

I rolled my eyes.[34]

He scooped up an entire ball of sorbet and jammed it in his mouth. Orange dribbled down his chin. I almost punched him for hogging but we were at Beni's.[35]

Dad whipped a napkin at him. "A.J.!"

"It's okay, we'll be back tomorrow. You can order more."

My parents looked at me like I had a big announcement to make.

"Did my bracelets arrive?"

"Nope," A.J. said, like he even knew what they were.

---

[34] And assumed he was on drugs.

[35] No fighting.

I wondered if I had been nominated for the Phoenix Five but that was impossible since the ballots don't go out until April. "Did I get early acceptance to college?"

"Did you apply to college?" Mom asked.

"No."

A.J. lifted his Sprite.

"I got a job. A real one."

Mom and Dad exchanged a worried glance. They had been down this dead-end road before.

"Where?"

"Spencer BMW."

"The dealership?" Dad asked, shocked.

A.J. nodded, his green eyes extra bright. As if the internal electric bill had been paid and the power was back on.

"What will you be doing, exactly?" Mom asked, applying her signature red lipstick.

"Selling."

"Cars?" Dad asked.

"No, stolen jewelry."

"A.J.!"

"Of course, cars. They just got the M3 GTR. Mr. Spencer said I'll get a thousand dollars on top of my commission if I sell it before the end of October. I'm dying to test that thing."

Dad handed Oskar his Visa, then leaned toward the center of the table. "How did you get such a good ... opportunity?"

"I know Mr. Spencer from the car wash. He requested me all the time 'cause I treated his M3 like an object of beauty, not

151

a car. I told him that's because it is an object of beauty and a pleasure to wash."

"Vomit," I said.

"He gave me his card and told me to keep in touch. I did."

My parents stood up to hug A.J.

"Oskar, looks like we'll be seeing you tomorrow," Dad said.

"Congratulations, Vanessa," said the waiter.

"It's me this time," A.J. announced.

Oskar gripped his chest and stumbled backward like he was having a heart attack. Then he hugged my brother too. It was hilarious.

Ver? I didn't feel jealous at all. How could I? Everyone was legitimately happy and A.J. was finally doing something he cared about. Anyway, it's just as hard to stay in trouble as it is to stay out of it, and we both needed the break.

> *Instead of asking "what's the problem?" ask "what's the creative opportunity?"*
>
> —Deepak Chopra

Lily

Sunday, September 23, 2012

While my hands were on Duffy's body, sparks, akin to static-electricity-sweater-shocks, passed between us. If I had been blessed with Sheridan Spencer's wardrobe or a fetching opening line, I could have fanned those sparks into a flame. But it had been thirteen days since the armpit hoist, and only one measly spark remained. I had to revive the passion or risk losing it forever. I had to get jeans.

Ideally, I would have been watering the grass in my new denims when the dusty 4Runner returned. Duffy would be unloading the camping gear when I caught his eye. He'd wonder if dehydration was having its way with his mind because girls like this don't go unnoticed. He'd drop his fishing pole to the driveway and get swept up in the rip current of love at first sight. Mr. Duffy would ask where he was floating off to. Then insist he come back and help. Duffy wouldn't. He couldn't. The pull would be too powerful. He'd finally be close enough to inhale my exhales. He'd say, nice jeans. I'd say, nice lips. He'd place his hand on his heart, for the words to describe his feelings would have escaped him. He'd lean toward me for a kiss. I'd meet him halfway. Then I'd nail him with the hose and we'd crack up.

This should have been our story. But Vanessa Riley had my Algebra quiz, which messed it all up. I couldn't get my A+ money without my A+. I couldn't get my seduction jeans without my money. And I couldn't get Duffy without those jeans.

I wanted to skate to her house and get the quiz but Blake made me call instead. He said showing up when I hardly knew the girl made me look like a stalker. I thought calling was more stalker-ish. Blake disagreed. I almost said, "I should know what stalking is because I am a stalker." But I didn't. I just flopped down on my bed beside Blake and dialed.

I listened to the rings and prayed Vanessa would answer.

"What if she isn't home?"

"Leave a message."

"What if she says she'll bring it to school tomorrow?"

"Say you need it today."

I hung up.

"She'll think I'm a freak."

"So."

"So, what if she asks why I need it so badly?"

"Tell her."

"Tell her what? That I was rejected by the style club? That I can't buy anything flattering unless I pay for it myself? I can't tell her that!"

"Why?" Blake asked, flipping through my X–Y encyclopedia. Yep, I still use encyclopedias. They're faster than dial-up.

"Because Vanessa Riley is perfect."

"Then why did she get a B-plus on the Algebra quiz?"

"Valid."

I dialed again. My heart, desperate for me to reconsider, thumped harder. I swiped a puff off Blake's inhaler.

"Lil, you have social anxiety, not asthma!" he said, reaching for it. I licked it.

"Ew, don't give me your Coxsackie," he squealed, wiping the inhaler on his Ashcroft plaid.

"You're the one with Coxsackie!"

"S'cuse me?" Vanessa said.

"Oh god. No. Not you. Sorry. I was talking to Blake and—"

"Blake?"

"Yeah, hi, it's Lily."

Blake was cracking up and I was trying not to but I couldn't help it.

"What's so funny?"

"Sorry. It's nothing." I leg-swiped Blake off the bed. He fell with a thud, which cracked us up all over again.

"If nothing's so funny, why are you laughing?"

"It's just that for some reason the word 'Coxsackie' kills us. And Blake said it right when you picked up the—"

"The disease kills more than you two," she said.

"Huh?"

"My grandpa had Coxsackie." She sniffled. *"Had."*

The line went dead.

My blood stopped mid-flow. Blake's brown cheeks faded to beige. We stared at the phone.

"This is all your fault!"

"How is it my fault?"

"You made me call her."

"You told her Coxsackie makes us laugh!"

"How was I supposed to know her grandpa—"

The phone rang. I made Blake answer.

"Kidding!" Vanessa shouted.

We all had a good laugh, at the end of which Blake bellowed, "Love this girl!"

We laughed for at least ten more minutes before Vanessa asked why I called.

Next thing I know she was at my house with the quiz and the three of us were off to the mall to buy me some discounted love jeans.

J.Crew was packed and Trike was in a tizzy, so we hit the food court. It was packed too, so Blake and I snagged a table while Vanessa went in search of kettle corn.

"I think she likes you."

"Easy, Emma," he said, accusing me of matchmaking, like the title character from Jane Austen's novel. (Homie humor.) "She's just being nice."

"Nice is offering to buy snacks," I said. "*Like* is everything else she's been doing."

"Proof."

"You have such good style, Blake. I've always wanted to skateboard, Blake. Blake, will you teach me, Blake? Blake, what was it like being homeschooled? Blake, you're so tanned. Blake—"

"Okay!"

"Can I please tell her you're dating Tr— Mike?"

"No!"

"Why?"

"Lil, I told you, I don't want to be known as the gay guy."

"I know, but do you want to be known as the straight guy?"

"I want to be known as Blake."

"It's cruel."

"What's cruel?"

"Leading her on."

"I'm not treating her any differently than—"

"Kettle corn!" Vanessa said, handing us our bags.

Blake glared at me. I blinked once: a promise not to tell.

IRONY ALERT! IRONY ALERT! IRONY ALERT!

What started out as me feeling bad for Vanessa ended up as me feeling worse for myself. Much worse.

Everyone who passed our table slowed to check her out. I wasn't totally surprised because her face is worthy of an extended look. Astroturf-green eyes. Curls that don't frizz. Butterscotch-colored skin. Cheekbones. She was wearing long sleeves so I know people weren't gawking because she's slutty. It's because she's beautiful. More beautiful than me. I wanted to punch her.

And then it hit me.

I, Lily Bader-Huffman-Duffy, have been admiring my reflection through Homie-colored lenses; lenses that had me thinking I was beautiful too. Because, in our group of seven, I was. Blake, Hamilton, and Legend are male. Wendi shaves her head for swim meets, Maple has a lazy eye, and Sylvie picks her pimples. In Homie world I was the hot one. But I live in Pub world now. Where I'm "meh" at best.

Suddenly, this expedition seemed futile. Guys like Duffy want exotic girls like Vanessa or actress-pretty types like Sheridan. I know this because I never see Duffys with Lilys. And no amount of denim will change that.

Not that it mattered. The jeans never happened. We went back to J.Crew. Blake told Trike the Coxsackie story, which made everyone laugh all over again, everyone but Trike. He just stood there, arms folded, leg jutted, face pinched as if he'd just chugged sour milk. He obviously felt left out, or threatened, or resentful, because he claimed "employee discounts" were an urban legend, then pivoted toward the "Looks We Love" display in search of something to fold.

"Mike!" Blake said, hurrying after him.

Vanessa thought nothing of the lovers' quarrel. She assumed they were two buddies in a scrap and agreed that we should wait for Blake outside.

Twenty minutes later I suggested we spend my twenty on a movie. Something formulaic and meaningless. Perfect for Pub.

She peeked inside the store. "Nah. I should get back and study for AP World History."

"Bummer."

"Did you study already?" Vanessa asked.

"I'll look over my notes during lunch or something."

"Veritas? That's all you do?"

I shrugged like it was no big deal because it wasn't.

"Wow."

I slipped out from under her awestruck gaze and feigned interest in the Crabtree and Evelyn's fall-hued candles.

"What's it like being so naturally smart?" Vanessa asked.

What's it like being so naturally pretty? I wanted to ask. But Blake showed up and suggested we see a movie.

"Can't," I said. "Vanessa has to stu—"

"Sure!"

"Really?"

"You're right, Lily. We can study at lunch."

I'm in bed now. I just kicked off my covers because the thought of cramming with Vanessa fills me with warmth. I made a Pub friend. A smart one. A funny one. A beautiful one. I want to tell her the truth about Blake. I made a promise, though, so I won't. Still. It's going to be hard watching her waste feelings on a guy who will never like her back. I know. I watch myself do it every day and it's seriously pathetic.

Lily Bader-Huffman-Duffy

Vanessa

September 23rd, aka Best Day Ever!

Have to hurry. We're leaving for Beni's in five. Love you, A.J.!!!

I digress...

Today started with a prank call from Lily and Blake. Coincidentally, I had just completed my research[36] when they called. So, I wiped my tears away, put extra ointment on my arms, and called right back with a sense of humor. And guess what? It worked![37] Blake actually said he loved me. I'm not kidding. He really said that.

----

[36] Googled "what boys look for in a girl?" Sense of humor is key.

[37] Massive understatement.

This leads me to three conclusions:

1) The prank was his idea but he had Lily[38] call because he was shy. Classic boy behavior.
2) He likes me.
3) His friend Mike may be a problem.

I sensed him checking me out the moment we were introduced. After Blake told him about the Coxsackie thing I added the "Love this girl" part. After that Mike got all testosterone-y. My guess? He realized Blake and I have chemistry. Who knows, maybe they have a history of liking the same girls. Maybe Mike always loses to Blake. A natural assumption, because if hotness was graded, Blake would have a 4.0 average and Mike would be struggling to maintain a 2.75.

I wanted to ask Lily for some backstory but I didn't want her to think I was using her to get to Blake. Because I'm not...[39]

Mom's calling. Time to leave for dinner. I'll get serious about studying tomorrow.

(Sorry, no time for a quote.)

....

[38] I am not going to call her a "Before" picture anymore. We had fun today. Do I still suspect she may be trying to sabotage my GPA? Yes. So I will watch her closely.

[39] ...anymore. (See above footnote for further explanation.)

Sheridan

9.24.12

EXT. NOBLE HIGH PICKUP CURB—LATE AFTERNOON.

It's raining. Campus is empty. MOM's car battery died. DAD is training a new salesman. According to the note SHERIDAN got from the office someone will be here eventually.

SHERIDAN's black dress is soaked. Too numb to care, she sits on the bench by the Pick and Flick. The sky is stormy. She puts quill to paper.

FLASHBACK. LAST WEDNESDAY.

I slept with the *Wicked* soundtrack (original cast recording) under my pillow and woke feeling refreshed and prepared for my audition. My Glinda glitter gown had been fluffed, my hair curled to perk-fection, and my throat coated in honey.

There were about twenty-five people in the Starlight Auditorium when Audri and I arrived. So I chose two seats in the front to keep us from analyzing the competition and getting all intimidated. Audri kept turning around anyway. I assumed she was nervous and/or looking for Mr. Kimball until I heard:

Owdeee! (Octavia.)

What is she doing here? (Me.)

Audri was too busy waving to answer.

I can't believe she came. (Audri to me.) *I can't believe you came!* (Audri to Octavia.)

A deal's a deal. (Octavia, bouncing over in her knee-high Converse.)

What deal? (Me.)

Octavia lowered her celery butt onto the arm of "Owdie's" chair and angled her fat-free torso toward my best friend.

Oh m'gad, Sheridan, you have to hear this. (Audri, leaning over Octavia's lap.) *So O shows up in the cafeteria today all angry and stuff because—*

Wait, didn't you say she has tennis practice at lunch? (I said it like this because I wanted "O" to know how creepy it feels to be talked about like you're not there when you are.)

She does. That's the point. Cat, her doubles partner, bailed because Octavia was hogging the ball.

Mine, mine, mine. (Octavia.) *Mine, mine, mine.* (Audri.) *Mine, mine, mine.* (Both.)

Oh m'gad, so hilar. (Audri, uttering "hilar" for the first time ever.) *Anyway, she asked me to be her new partner and—*

You? (I said like it was the most outrageous thing ever. Because it was.) *Talk about "hilar"! Did you say no?*

I said only if you try out for Wicked.

What? (Me.) *Why would you say that?*

Because she thought I'd say no. But I didn't. Obviously. (Octavia.)

Do you even act?

I've dabbled.

Dabbled? What does that mean?

It means I've tried it.

I know what dabbled means. But what does it mean in terms of acting?

It means I was in a play once and thought it was boring so I took up tennis.

Bor-ing? How can you say—

So the deal is if Octavia gets a part in the play, I'll try out for the tennis team. How hilar is that? (Audri.)

I've heard more hilar.

Octavia's back was now more like those cubicle walls in my dad's office with me on one side and Audri on the other. They started whispering. I closed my eyes so they'd think I was getting into character, but really I was channeling a canine for maximum hearing. It worked. Octavia was telling Audri about her crush, Logan.

We talked two times in the last five days. Not small talk, either.

Big talk...remember, I told you how I wished him luck before his basketball tryout last Friday...turns out he didn't make it because Hudson had his dad buy him a spot on the team...Logan figured it out and busted the whole scam wide open...now he's on...he told me today...anyway, can you believe he told me all of that?... good sign, right?...have a party when my parents go to New York...perfect excuse to invite him over and—

It's your fault he didn't make the team. (Me.)

Sher! (Audri.)

Come on, Audri, you know it's true.

She pulled off her glasses and cleaned a spot that wasn't there.

'Scuse me? (Octavia.) *How is that my fault?*

You said good luck. (Audri.)

You never wish someone good luck before an audition. Sports or otherwise. (Me.)

Why?

You say break a leg. (Audri.)

Why would I say that?

Um, ever heard of a superstition? (Me. Condescending.)

She scratched her airhead. I took that as a no.

During curtain call, when actors bow or curtsy, they place one foot behind the other and bend at the knee, thus "breaking" the line of the leg.

And they only bow when people are clapping so it means they did well. (Audri.) *So breaking a leg is a good thing.*

But he's a basketball player. He doesn't bow.

167

And he probably never will, thanks to you. (Me.)

Mr. Kimball clapped once to announce himself and twice for silence. He looked at his clipboard and began calling hopefuls to the stage and having them sing. There were some solid contenders in the mix but no one as good as me. I wasn't being conceited. Just real.

When Mr. Kimball said *Sheridan Spencer* I literally jumped. I was that ready.

Break a leg! (Audri.)

Thanks. (Me.)

I closed my eyes and waited for Kristin Chenoweth to appear. The golden blond hair came first, then the high-beam smile, then—

GOOD LUCK! (Octavia.)

Audri gasped.

Kristin's forming image disintegrated into an anthill of glitter.

Uh-oh. (Mr. Kimball, glancing up at the theater lights to make sure they were secure.)

Always the professional, I took a steadying breath and somehow managed to sing "Popular" perfectly. The proof was in the applause.

I couldn't help wondering if somehow my talent was God herself. I mean, who—other than the Great Almighty—could triumph after "good luck's" deadly kiss? I was touched by an angel.

At least that's what I thought until Octavia auditioned with

"Popular" too. If I was touched by an angel, that lucky devil was groped.

Everyone, including Mr. Kimball, cheered. I clenched my jaw and silently blamed Audri for allowing this demonic parasite to infiltrate our lives.

Hey, Sheridan. (Parasite, in my face.) *That play I dabbled in? It was* Wicked. Then she grabbed her Big Cat bag, hooked it over her shoulder, and before leaving said, *I was Glinda. Oh, see you on the court, Owdee.*

BACK TO PRESENT DAY. STILL RAINING. STILL SOAKED. STILL NUMB TO IT ALL.

The most heinous part of this whole ordeal? Mr. Kimball posted the cast list on Friday. Audri did not make Glinda's understudy. She got Elphaba. The bad witch. The lead. The role I played last year. Octavia got Glinda. And I, Sheridan Spencer, have been cast as Glinda's underst—

Dad's here.

To Be Continued . . .

END SCENE.

169

INT. BMW M5—LATE AFTERNOON.

Dad is going on about some new salesman he hired—a junior at Noble. Someone who reminds him of himself when he was starting out. I keep saying *cool* and *sounds great* but I'm journaling instead. Duffy biked up to the Pick and Flick right when Dad pulled up, and even though I get carsick I have to put quill to paper while our conversation is still fresh in my head.

Were you on vacation? (Me.)

No, why?

You weren't in English today and you're all tanned.

It's not a tan. I have a fever.

Then why are you here? School's over.

Delivering a check to my basketball coach.

Why did you ride your bike in the rain if you're sick?

I don't have a driver's license. (Duffy.) *Why do you look like you were at a funeral?*

I was.

Whose?

My own.

We laughed.

Why are we asking each other so many questions? (Him.)

Why do you think?

We laughed again.

Where are you going now? (Him, looking at my dad's car.)

To sing show tunes for my old Barbies.

Break a leg. (Him.)

Did you just say 'break a leg'?

170

Yeah, sorry. I'm kinda superstitious. It means—
I know what it means.

Must stop writing. Feel carsick.

Okay, better. Anyway, I can't believe Duffy knew what break a—

Just puked.
I wish I could channel the end of a movie and fade out.

To Be Continued…
END SCENE.

DUFFY

Monday

Feeling = Slick.

I had no choice.

My parents are in the red. Amelia lectured me on "the character-building benefits of delayed gratification" and Bubbie Libby has $20 Canadian. Mandy could get me an interview at Abercrombie, but I needed the money right away.

ME: Can Gardner help?

MANDY: His parents are in the red too.

ME: Then how is he rolling in green?

MANDY: He works.

ME: Where? Italian *Vogue*?

Mandy looked impressed by my reference. I only knew *Vogue* came in Italian because the magazine was on her desk with a ton of junk from CVS.

MANDY: Why don't you play on the freshman team?

ME: Why don't you date Coops?

Mandy was on her bed. She knocked over a bottle of yellow nail polish when I said that.

MANDY: Seriously?

ME: Seriously, what?

MANDY: Leaving Varsity to play Freshman is like me dumping Gardner for *Coops*?

ME: Worse.

MANDY: Fine.

She picked up her cell with her palms and said, "Call G-licious."

SIRI: Cal-ling Gee-liss-i-us.

She put Gardner on speakerphone and told him I needed money. Gardner made me swear on my basketball career that I would never tell another living human what he was about to tell me.

ME: I swear.

He said he could get me the money if I skipped school on Monday.

ME: No prob.

GARDNER: Meet me at Regal Park. 8:00 AM. No hoodies or taped-up shoes. You sleep in a home, not a refrigerator box. Dress like it. Mandy, take me off speaker.

My sister poked the phone with her elbow and brought it to her ear. Her hair got stuck in her wet nail polish.

MANDY: Yeah . . . I can pull some stuff from Abercrombie . . . he will . . . he won't . . . yes you can trust him . . . okay . . . thanks G-lish . . . L Y 2 . . .

Feeling = Mad at my parents.

If they weren't in the red I would have told Gardner I'd rather look like I came from a box than an Abercrombie sale. I wouldn't have spent my Sunday at the mall with Mandy—where I had to hide from Lily, Vanessa, and Blake so they wouldn't see me with shopping bags covered in naked dudes. And I definitely would not have accepted this slick new job. Correction. Slick new "lifestyle."

That's how Anton, my "style sensei," suggests I "view" this "shopportunity."

Anton is the owner of Trendemic. Trendemic is "a marketing company that turns products into trends and designers into millionaires."

I spent five hours in his secret *Mission: Impossible* headquarters. I was interviewed, measured, weighed, photographed, spray tanned, manicured, and allergy tested. Then I was hired. Correction. "Contracted."

ANTON: As of today you are no longer Andrew Duffy. You are an "It Guy." A human billboard. A tastemaker. A 3-D, HD, breathing advurt-es-mint.

ME: Huh?

ANTON: Your job is to model clothes by avant-garde designers. Enjoy revolutionary snack foods and savor revolutionary drinks in public. Scent your body parts with mists that conjure images of far-off places. Use our sporting gear, hair products, accessories, and high-tech footwear in the presence of your wealthy peers. Make it look...sexy. Crucial for social success. A cinch to buy. Because the more they spend, my accessibly handsome It Guy, the more you make.

The lights dimmed. Video started to play on the LCD screen behind his desk. Italian *Vogue*–type clothes, veggie chips in metallic bags, fur-covered sunglasses...I started to sweat through my Abercrombie Henley. (Why's it called a Henley?) My pits smelled like baby powder because I ran out of deodorant in the summer so I've been using Mandy's. Thinking about the new things I was going to smell like made me sweat even more.

The freak show ended and the lights came back on.

ME: I have to wear that stuff?

ANTON: Inspiring, isn't it? Each week a box will arrive at your house with the latest and greatest. Wear it, eat it, drink it, spritz it and they will come.

ME: Who will?

ANTON: The fourteen-to-twenty-five-year-old males.

ME: For what?

ANTON: For what you have. They'll compliment you. You tell them you have a hookup. You can get them the same thing at a discounted rate. Give them the coupon

175

code that arrives with the shipment and send them to the specified website address. They buy it. You get twenty percent. Girls too. Show them our female brands and I'll give you twenty percent of that too.

ME: The thing is, Anton—

ANTON: Sensei.

ME: Sensei, I need twenty-five hundred today.

ANTON: Sign this contract and I will give you an advance. You're sixteen, right?

ME: Actually, I'm only—

ANTON: Of course you are.

He gave me a stack of papers and told me to take my time reading them.

I couldn't concentrate. All I could think about was showing up at school in tight red jeans and a white belt. Cowhide blazers and shirts with different colored buttons. Logos! What would Hud and Coops say? They'd know something was up. What would I tell them? What could I tell them? I had to walk away. I had to run.

How could I, though? The only thing I ever wanted was to play Varsity. If I quit, Hud and Coops would know something was up and it's not like I could tell them about the bankrupt thing. I promised my dad.

I told myself that this job is temporary. I could make the money back in a few weeks and then It-quit. Anyway, Dennis Rodman wore lipstick. He dyed his hair green. He dressed like a bride. He pierced his face. And he was inducted into the Basketball Hall of Fame, so.

I signed all twenty pages. Now I'm in the red too.

Anton gave me the check and I rushed it over to Coach Bammer. He was afraid I wouldn't show. He asked me why I looked tanned. I told him I had a fever. Same thing I told Sheridan when I saw her. I wanted to tell her the truth. She seems easy to talk to. But I can't. I signed a contract. I have no clue what it says but I'm sure keeping this quiet is in there.

Feeling = Hall of Fame here I come.

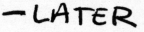

Lily

Wednesday, September 26, 2012

On our way to Brooklyn for a belated Rosh Hashanah dinner at Aunt Laura's. Goodbye 5772 and hello 5773! This new year couldn't have come at a better time. So what if it's the Jewish one and we're celebrating ten days late because Uncle Eli had the stomach flu? A fresh start is a fresh start. And oy, do I need one.

Vanessa and I met on Monday to study for our AP World History test. Only we kind of forgot the studying part. Not to say that the rise and achievements of African civilizations, including but not limited to Axum, Ghana, Kush, Mali, Nubia, and Songhai, are not important. They are. Especially when considering the reasons for their decline. But I already knew about animism and trade systems. What I needed to learn was how to be normal.

My "in" came when Vanessa asked how I got so smart. I told her about my Homie past. I thought she would look at me all weird after that but she said I was lucky because I know so much. I said she was luckier because she's pretty and everyone likes her.

"Looks are one thing, nothing I can do about that. But popularity? That can be taught."

"I wish."

"Trust me," she muttered. "It's easier than getting A's, that's for sure."

"Go on."

Astroturf-green eyes alight, Vanessa leaned across the table and whispered, "Popularity can be achieved in five simple steps."

I swept our binders to the floor. Finally, information I could use.

"One: Be friendly and outgoing. Smile even if you are unhappy. Say things like, 'That point you made in class? So true!' or 'Mind if I take your picture for my style blog?' or 'Who does your extensions? . . . What do you mean they're not extensions? Hair like that cannot be real!'

"Two: Stay under the radar. Don't attract attention. Attention leads to gossip.

"Three: Be a good listener. Ask questions. Keep unpopular opinions to yourself.

"Four: Don't be a know-it-all. Don't hog the ball. Don't brag about good grades or awards. Stay humble.

"Five: Avoid weird clothes or hairstyles that inspire gossip.

Stick with stylish, modest outfits. Dress like the people you are trying to befriend. Eat the same foods and drink the same drinks."

Vanessa leaned back, satisfied. "Easy, right?"

"That's it?"

"No. I need to cite my source. I found steps one through three at w-w-w-dot—"

"It's okay," I said, cutting her off. I didn't care where she got my new toy. I just wanted to play with it.

I rolled it around and studied it from all angles. It was so simple—and the exact opposite of everything my mother taught me—so it had to work.

"I can do this," I said. "Everything but step five. My parents are freaks about money."

"Dip into your computer fund you're always talking about," Vanessa said. "Buy a few versatile basics and you're done."

She was right. A few A+'s and I'd replenish in no time.

Unfortunately, I got an A- on the AP World History test and Vanessa got a B. But we did end up going to the mall again with Blake, which seemed to cheer her up. Trike even apologized for his bad mood on Sunday. He asked for our home addresses so he could mail us some Friends and Family discount vouchers and started pulling outfits for me.

Blake and Vanessa waited outside the fitting room while I tried everything on. Every time I came out Vanessa said something about my cute body and how she had no clue I was so tiny. Blake agreed.

I paid $267.72 for two pairs of skinny jeans and a mint-green tank top from the sale rack.

"As long as your wallet is open—" Blake started.

"What?"

He mimed combing his hair. I hadn't anticipated the extra expense of a brush but it was worth it. I spent $298.49 and I look like a million bucks. How's that for a good investment?

We just pulled into Aunt Laura's driveway. I am not wearing my new clothes. Mom would pull me from Pub if she knew I tapped my savings for clothes. She would also pull me if she knew about the A-.

But all of that is so 5772. Why go there?

Shalom.

Lily Bader-Huffman-Duffy

Jagger

Sept. 27.

I signed up for the Noble debate team.

Judge.

You won't be the first.

I'm a lanky dude with shaggy hair. I dwell on the edge of society. I don't dress to impress but to avoid arrest. Dudes like me are usually artists or rock stars. Poets or protesters. Not members of the debate team. Because debates are arguments with rules. And Jagger doesn't do rules.

I do scholarships though.

Colleges don't give those away to kids who play guitar in the garage. Besides, there is no garage at the pet store. Just a storage cube where Randy keeps the bugs and rodents I feed to bigger bugs and rodents.

The arts are for rich kids who can afford to take risks.

Dudes like me have to make a choice.

Feed your soul or your stomach?

Debate *that*.

Today's topic was the death penalty.

We were about to pick sides when Vanessa Riley walks in. A late sign-up. Most of the guys looked at each other because she's pretty. They can have her. I'm more of a quirk-man. Mr. Cannon welcomed her and asked if she'd like to hit the ground running.

She surprised us all and said sure, I'll speak for the proposition.

Mr. Cannon asked who wanted to take the opposition.

Guys wanted to date, not debate, girls like Vanessa. So I volunteered.

I'd rather eat dog biscuits for Christmas than be the center of attention. But this was more than a topic. It was the story of my life—a story ending with my parents' deaths.

I walked to the podium. Chairs creaked. Spectators were settling in for what promised to be an entertaining match. Beauty versus Beast.

Beauty proved to be a worthy opponent.

Her arguments for the death penalty:

- Important tool to preserve law and order.

- Deters crime.
- Costs the taxpayers less than life imprisonment.
- Honors the victim.
- Ensures this criminal will never be back on the streets.

My arguments against the death penalty:
- Criminals don't consider punishment when they commit their crimes so it's not a deterrent.
- Wrongly gives the government the power to take human life.
- Perpetuates social injustice by targeting people of color and low incomes.
- Lethal injection is the easy way out. Jail is worse.

Turns out Beauty had brains but Beast had heart.

It was time for the closing rebuttal.

Beauty did a fine job summing up her argument. I did the same. And then I added this:

My mother and father are on death row. They avenged a minor who was the victim of a heinous bully attack. Now they are paying for it with their lives. And mine. On June 1, 2014, I will be an orphan. This is why I am opposed to the death penalty.

The spectators were still.

Then they were not. They cheered and whistled. I won.

Everyone in the club had questions. Condolences. Invitations to eat with their families. I accepted them all.

Vanessa ran for the door.

I went to look for her but found Audri instead.

She was wearing a yellow tennis skirt and a white tank top. I forgot about Vanessa.

Audri joined the tennis team. We won't be able to have lunch together because that's when her partner likes to practice.

She said we'll have to find other times to hang out.

I offered her a ride home on my bike.

She accepted.

I gave her my seat and stood behind her, pedaling. Her hair blew against my face. I smelled strawberries. I'd rather look at Audri's blue glasses than Vanessa's green eyes.

We stood outside her house for a while. She didn't want to go in. She had just spent the weekend with her dad but she still missed him. She missed having him at home. She cried.

She apologized for crying. I told her not to. I know what it's like to miss family. I told her I cry about it sometimes too.

She asked if she could tell me something. Something she'd never told anyone. Not even her best friend Sheridan. I said of course.

Last March, on that crazy snow day, school closed early. Audri and Sheridan thought it would be fun to walk home in the storm so they didn't call home for a ride. Soaked and freezing, she hurried up the steps to her house. Her mom was home too. She could see her through the window. She was with a man in a suit. She couldn't see his face, only his back. Still, it was obvious what they were doing. Audri took their picture with her phone and then hid in the garage until he left. She sat on the washing machine, shivering and crying for two hours.

She didn't tell her mother what she saw. Telling her would mean talking to her, and she never wanted to speak to her again. So Audri printed the picture and mailed it anonymously to her father. She hoped they would talk about it, realize it was a misunderstanding, and everything would be fine.

It wasn't.

Her parents fought for months.

Her father moved out.

Audri blames herself.

Time to feed the pets.

-J

Having a hard time falling asleep.

I can't believe Audri told me her biggest secret.

I wish I could tell her mine.

Vanessa

September 27th

OhmygodOhmygodOhmygodOhmygodOhmygodOhmygod
  Ohmygod
  Ohmygod
  Ohmygod
  Ohmygod
  Ohmygod
  Ohmygod
  Ohmygod
  Ohmygod
  OH MY GOD!

I am at Starbucks decompressing with a decaf caramel latte. Why? Because caffeine would detonate my heart.[40] Instead of journaling on a worn velvet couch by a fake fireplace, I should be under police protection. Far away in another town with a new name and a wig. I could be tortured for what I know. Arrested. But I won't be. Because I won't use this classified information to my advantage. Even though I want to. Even though I could.

STOP THINKING ABOUT IT, VANESSA! WRITE ABOUT SOMETHING ELSE. WRITE ABOUT BLAKE.

Blake is my catnip. He makes me feel giddy and playful. I am a spoon sinking into his hot fudge eyes, scraping the edges for every last bit of sweetness I can get.[41] And Lily isn't like any girl I've ever met. She makes me want to be less . . . normal. In a good way. Her best friend is a boy. She never has to study. She skateboards and eats special food and wears highlighter on her nails because she doesn't want to waste her computer money on cosmetics. Getting to know them has been full of wonder and excitement. A treasure chest full of hope for a super-fun tomorrow. Like discovering a cure or a new country. Christopher Columbus, I know the feeling.

My EKG may be up but my GPA is down. Way down. Columbus's would be too if he had to choose between island

---

[40] Seriously, sentences like this should be graded.

[41] Another great metaphor.

hopping and reviewing his notes on animism. Point is, the Good Grade Ship has sailed off without me.

UGH, HOW DID I GET BACK TO GRADES???? FINE. I SURRENDER. I'M GOING TO WRITE ABOUT THE THING I DON'T WANT TO THINK ABOUT. MAYBE THAT WILL MAKE ME STOP THINKING ABOUT IT...

I joined the debate team to compensate for my weak grades. DT looks great on college applications and I know how to argue. After all, fighting is the soundtrack of my life.[42]

The club was all boys. They sat up taller when I walked in. At least one was gearing up to flirt. I couldn't exactly come right out and tell them I'm taken because, technically, it's not true.[43] Still, my heart was not on the auction block. Intimidating these potential suitors with my skill and confidence was the only way to ward them off. Thusly, I accepted Mr. Cannon's offer[44] to "hit the ground running."

Then the orphan stepped up. After arguing in favor of the death penalty I understood why he is called "the Orphan." News of his parents' imminent death was a lethal injection to my dignity. So I hit the ground running straight to Principal Alden's office to review alternative club options.

His secretary gave me a tissue and had me wait in his office. Apparently, he was grabbing a danish from the teachers' room.

....

[42] Another winner!

[43] ...Yet.

[44] In this case, "offer" means "dare."

One should never underestimate the power of an unexpected Christmas gift from a student. So I scanned the decor to home in on his taste. A framed photo of two Bernese mountain dogs on a hiking trail. A space needle of folders piled high on his desk. A navy cardigan on the back of his ergonomic chair. A list of students' names on his computer. Some I recognized. Most I didn't. I leaned closer. There were letters to the right of the names. Grades. *Our* grades. Grades that would determine our futures. Futures that could be changed with a keystroke. Or the touch of—

"Miss Riley," said Principal Alden, chewing. "Denise said you had some concerns. Something about your GPA?"

"Me? No. I'm fine. I, um, I just wanted to introduce myself," I stammered. "You know, personally."

He wiped his hands on his Dockers and then shook my hand. His was sticky. Mine was sweaty.

"This must be my lucky day," he said, more annoyed than flattered. "You're the seventh student who's come to kiss my caboose since lunch."

"I'm sorry?"

He tapped on the space bar of his computer. The names were gone. "There's going to be a lot of competition for the Principal's Award this year. A real nail-biter."

"Good, because I haven't had a manicure in weeks. All that studying..."

I bolted before he could look at me funny. Because, ver? I had no idea what I was saying. My jammed circuits could only process one thing—that list of grades.

One simple keystroke...one! That's all that stood between me and a 4.0. That and access to his office. Maybe a password. But A.J. could teach me to hack and—

STOP!

This is exactly the kind of thinking I need to avoid. Anyway, if A.J. keeps doing well at Spencer BMW, my grades won't matter as much. We've had Beni's two more times since I last wrote. So it's not like this very illegal opportunity is tempting me in the least. Because it's not. I'll work harder and smarter and I'll forget everything I just saw.

Starting now.

Think positive.[45]

—Deepak Chopra

---

[45] Not his greatest work. But effective nonetheless.

Sheridan

10.1.12

INT. STARLIGHT AUDITORIUM, THE WINGS—LATE AFTERNOON.

It's Monday, October 1st—the first day of blocking. SHERIDAN has learned so much already.

Being an understudy is underrated. I'm a ghost. Present but invisible. And, show of hands if you haven't dreamt of being invisible at some point? Mr. Kimball has been positioning and repositioning the leads for the past hour while I get to kick back in the wings and quill. Passive theater. Who knew?

In case you can't tell, I am channeling a good sport—specifically Leighton Meester, who plays Blair Waldorf on *Gossip Girl*. It's no secret that Blake Lively's Serena has a much better wardrobe. She gets boho's best while Leighton is candy-coated in unflattering blues and yellows. But does Leighton kick off her ballet flats and UGG off the set? No. She sucked it up for six straight seasons. She tasted that costume rainbow. Choked on it, even. But she still showed up. And so shall I.

Yesterday, Audri and I hung in the blue rocket for hours. It's this metal rocket ship on the playground in our gated community. We go there to have deep conversations. Usually around dinnertime when the little kids go home. The following was our deepest yet:

FLASHBACK.

I love this day. (Me.)

Why?

You're not at your dad's.

Yeah.

Do you like going there?

Only cuz I miss him.

Did you ever find out why they split up?

Audri pulled the pink lace on her sneakers so hard it broke.

Do you think they still love each other? (Me.)

Dunno.

Maybe we could do a musical fund-raiser or something. And use the money to buy them a trip to Paris.

What's that gonna do? (Audri.)

Make them fall in love again.

This is my life, Sher, not a romantic dramedy.

What's that supposed to mean?

Just—

What?

Nothing. (Audri.)

Tell me.

Fine. It means that everything with you is always so . . .

What?

. . . Dramatic!

"Dramatic" echoed through the rocket ship. It felt like a slap every time I heard it. Not because I thought being dramatic was bad. But because she did.

What's wrong with being dramatic? (Me.)

Nothing. It's just all you talk about.

So?

Sometimes I want to talk about other things.

Like what? Tennis?

She shrugged. *What's wrong with tennis?*

Nothing. I just never knew you were so into it.

I'm not sooo into it. (Audri making air quotes.) *But I like it. And I'm good.*

Do you like it more than acting?

No . . . I dunno . . . It's just something different.

Different like Octavia, the girl who cursed my audition?

She looked out at the treetops that lined the play area.

Or different like tight jeans and Jagger and everything else you're suddenly into.

She didn't answer. I got all quiet too because if I kept talking, I'd cry. So I just sat there for a minute, running my finger along the metal grating. The rustling leaves sounded the way my loneliness felt.

Does all this have to do with your parents' divorce? (Me, finally.)

All what?

Admit it, Audri. You've been weird lately.

Weird because I like a sport and a boy and someone other than you? That's not weird, Sher. It's normal.

Not for us.

(More silence.)

Most people have more than one friend or hobby.

So?

So, the only thing you have more than one of is personalities.

They're not personalities. They're personas. And I thought you liked them.

I do. I love them. But they're not enough.

I could channel more.

Audri smiled.

Sher, you're my best friend. I don't want that to change.

So why are you doing all of this?

I want variety. Like an ensemble cast instead of a one-woman show. Sometimes I get sick of acting and costumes and drama. It's nothing against you.

I always suspected Audri needed more. Which is why I tried so hard to give it to her. I just never thought that "more" meant more than me.

You okay?

My insides churned. *Yeah.*

I lived in fear of this "talk" for years. Not because I don't have other friends. I do. And I know my parents love me even though H&M get more attention. But Audri was *mine*. I didn't

197

have to share her with anyone....Anyway, that's what I thought. Mine...mine...mine.

Maybe I was more like Octavia than I thought.

So what do I do now? (Me, trying not to cry.)

Nothing. That's the point. Don't do anything. You be you and let me be me.

But what does that mean, exactly?

It means don't keep asking me when I got into tennis. And stop picking fights with Octavia. And don't look at me like some future star of 16 and Pregnant *because I like tight jeans, and don't roll your eyes when I mention Jagger and—*

Okay!

Oh, and try to be a good sport about this whole Wicked *thing. Let someone else be the lead for a change.*

I wanted to cry: Octavia doesn't need the lead like I do. She's never felt alone at her own birthday party or needed applause to feel seen. Or wanted to be someone else so desperately she's willing to make a career out of it. But I have! I *do*!

Not that I said any of that. Audri wanted less drama, not more.

I'm happy for you, Audri. You deserve the lead. But Octavia?

I know it's so random, right? She is good, though.

She's skilled. She's not talented and she's definitely not nuanced. That stuff makes a difference.

Just try to be nice.

I will.

One more thing. (Audri, pushing it.) *Stop acting like being the understudy is the worst thing in the world.*

Why?

I was the understudy—your understudy—and I was proud of that. I still am.

You should be. You were great.

Now it's your turn. Be great too.

We hugged. I felt empty and full at the same time. Mostly empty. But I am an actress. So I acted full.

BACK TO TODAY.

Dad drove Audri and me to school. His car is getting deep-cleaned because I got carsick in it when I tried to journal about Duffy. So he took the M3 GTR. He pretended it was something he had to do but I know he's been dying to drive it. Car crushes must be a guy thing because every dude was staring at us when we got out.

PAUSE.

Mr. Kimball just dismissed us.

END PAUSE. SHERIDAN is in HER ROOM.

I should be doing my Spanish homework but I had to put quill to paper because more happened after we were dismissed and I don't want to blank on the specifics.

FLASHBACK to the THEATER.

So after Mr. Kimball dismissed us, I exited the wings stage left and caught up with Octavia and Audri. They were planning a party. I didn't butt in because I wanted to give Audri space, but the ears want what the ears want. And my ears wanted to eavesdrop. So I trailed closely behind and learned the following:

Octavia's parents go away October 12th.

She wants to have a party so she can hang with Logan and Audri can hang with Jagger.

It will be a girl-ask-boy party. This gives them full control.

After this brief but informative exchange, Good Sport Meester congratulated Octavia on the lead. I said she deserved it. (Oscar, please!) Audri acknowledged my effort with a smile so it all seemed worth it, until Octavia responded.

Does this mean you're ready to admit I'm better than you?

I side-eyed Audri. She looked away. Good Sport Meester was about to Incredible Hulk into Chuck Bass, when Logan walked out of the gym and distracted us all.

Hey. (Octavia, poking the number on his jersey.) *We were just talking about you.*

Oh yeah?

She and Audri giggled.

Yeah.

'Bout what?

Nothing. More giggling.

Logan took a long drink at the water fountain and then wiped his mouth with the bottom of his Flames jersey. Then he turned to me.

Hey, Sheridan, you weren't kidding about that GTR.

Oh, you saw it?

Killer tail. (Logan.)

Awwww. I wuv those dogs! (Octavia.)

It's a car. (Me.)

I know. I call cars dogs. (Octavia.) *Does the GTR take gas? My cart is electric. It's totally green and—*

How fast does it go? (Logan.)

Thirty miles on a full charge. (Octavia.) *Owdee and I are going to knit bomb it in emerald yarn for* Wicked. *Sheridan, since you're my understudy, I'll let you knit some of it.*

No. The GTR. (Logan.) *How fast does it go?*

Does time travel interest you? (Me.)

Big-time.

Then test drive it.

I can?

Sure. I'll take you.

Octavia tugged his uniform. *Looks like you made the basketball team.*

Yeah.

So cool.

Yep.

I told Logan to write his number in my journal. He did.

Great. I'll call you later.

Don't forget.

I won't.

He went back into the gym. I tore out the page with his number and folded it into a tiny rectangle. Octavia glared at me as I stuffed it in the back pocket of my jeans and walked my pear-shaped butt down the hall.

I wanted to shout: *You break my heart, I'll break yours!* But I didn't. That's the kind of thing a jealous understudy would say. And Sheridan Spencer is no one's understudy.

To Be Continued ...

END SCENE.

DUFFY

Wednesday

Feeling = Slack.

I forgot all about this journal until Coops started bragging that he finished his. I almost said filling a journal with feelings is nothing to brag about. But the guy is in a Darth Vader boot so what else is he gonna do. So I said *cool*. Even though it isn't.

My classes are getting hard but the Flames have already played (and won!) two games. So even if I had feelings, I haven't had time to think about them. Unless feeling good counts. Because I've been feeling that. Especially after we played (and killed!) Cresskill. It was an away game but Coach Bammer ran a live feed on the Noble site so everyone back at school saw my winning shot. They also saw the other eighteen points I scored. The next day I got so many high fives it hurt to dribble. Coach Bammer was talking me up to the team during Monday's practice. Logo got so bent over it he walked out of the gym. He said he was going to get a drink of water even though there's a Dasani machine next to the bleachers and Steve Bowman offered him a dollar.

Another thing I forgot about was that box from Trendemic. Then I got this:

From: APryce@Trendemic_It.com
Subject: First and Last Warning
Date: October 3, 2012
To: It Guy #71470

Start selling.

Anton Pryce
Tastemaker. Style Sensei. Couture Connoisseur.

Then I saw an email that my *SI* subscription is about to run out so I dealt with that and forgot about the box all over again.

I just opened it.

Feeling = There is no way I am going to wear any of the following items to Noble.

- Black skinny jeans with neon glow-in-the-dark graffiti written all over them. It says "Tagged, you're it" on the butt.

- A black turtleneck sweater with white polka dots.
- A white V-neck with fake blood smeared all over the front. It says HEARTBREAKER on the back.
- A denim jacket covered in studs.
- Suspenders made of bicycle chains.
- Argyle socks with mini rabbit's feet dangling off the back.
- Gold basketball high-tops with black laces.
- Six cans of Sweat Energy Drink.
- Animaul unisex pheromone spray and body wash. (Whatever that is.)
- Mirrored sunglasses. Also in gold.

I locked my door and dumped it on my bed. Each item came with a code and product description. Not that I read them. I knew what these things were made to do: Destroy me.

Feeling = Two hours later and there's still no way I am ever going to wear this stuff to Noble.

Besides, my parents have no clue about this job. They think Coach Bammer is giving me a free ride because I'm so good and he didn't want to lose me. They wanted to thank him. I begged them not to. I said I promised it would be our secret. Since he could get fired for giving free rides. They agreed not to mention it but said they'd sponsor the Flames the minute they were back on their feet. I said he would appreciate that.

So I came up with a plan. I'd take the sprays and drinks to school and wear the clothes to other neighborhoods. Faraway ones. Ones that don't have high school basketball teams or anyone who knows my family.

Feeling = Lying gets easier with practice.

Greg is here. Flames play Summit tonight. Home game. Should be epic. I'll bring some Sweat.

Later.

Back from the game. 56–32 Flames. Weirdest night of my entire life. I wish I could tell someone.

Greg was honking. My high-tops weren't on the front porch where I left them. No one in my family had seen them. I asked twice. I looked everywhere. Greg kept honking.

Feeling = Who keeps taking my shoes???

I had no choice. I grabbed the gold Trendemic ones. Greg laughed at me the entire way to school. I wanted to tell him the shoes were a dare but I couldn't. So I said I was wearing them for charity.

GREG: What charity?

ME: Uh, you know how breast cancer has that pink ribbon? This one has gold shoes.

(I only know about the pink ribbons because the 3Ms tied them in their hair for the breast cancer dance-a-thon last year and their picture is still on our fridge. Coops tried to steal it twice.)

GREG: What's it called?

ME: Uh, the money goes to poor kids.

GREG: Which ones?

ME: The ones who can't play basketball.

GREG: Why can't they play?

ME: They're poor.

Greg laughed.

ME: Dude, it's not funny.

It was worse when I got to school. When Hud and Coops weren't cracking up they were calling me slick. Logo told everyone I was endorsed by Beyoncé. And when our teams shook hands the Summit guys wore sunglasses to cut the glare. I was trying my best to ignore the backlash but it was getting hard. I missed a few easy shots because of the heckling. We were down by twelve points. Bammer actually benched me for being a distraction. That's when Greg called a time-out. He walked to the center of the court and told everyone I was wearing the shoes for charity.

Their laughs turned to applause, which turned into me getting back in the game which turned into us winning. After the game I was mobbed. Everyone except Logo wanted a pair of "Duffys." I handed out the promo code and the website. A few of them balked at the $175 price tag but I reminded them it was for a good cause. Luckily, no one asked what it was. I was so busy selling shoes I forgot about the Sweat. Which was good because I ended up leaving the six-pack on the porch when I went to look for my shoes.

Greg dropped me off after the game. I didn't want to leave my "Duffys" outside in case someone stole them and Mom would have killed me if she saw me wearing them inside. So I snuck in through the back door.

BUBBIE: Andrew honey, is that you?

ME: Yeah.

BUBBIE: Come here. I want you to meet someone.

ME: One second.

BUBBIE: I'm old. I might not make it another second. Now.

I tried to kick off my Duffys.

BUBBIE: Your parents are out with the Wassermans. You can keep the shoes on.

Feeling = How does she always know?

Bubbie was in the kitchen drinking a beer with the Lily girl from school. Lily wasn't drinking beer though. She was drinking Sweat. Her cheeks looked sunburned and her lips were shiny. She looked cuter than she did the day that I Wiped. I think she brushed her hair.

BUBBIE: I want you to meet our neighbor, Lindsey.

LILY: Lily.

BUBBIE: She's Jewish.

ME: Right on.

LILY: Nice shoes.

ME: Long story.

LILY: I like them.

ME: Really?

LILY: Yeah.

BUBBIE: They're unsightly.

LILY: Did the Flames win tonight?

ME: Yup.

BUBBIE: Lindsey is our dog walker.

We laughed at Bubbie's mistake but didn't bother correcting her.

ME: Who hired you?

BUBBIE: I did. Such a nice Jewish girl.

ME: I thought you said you don't have any money.

BUBBIE: I have for some things, not others.

Lily held up the red-and-pink can of Sweat and asked if we recycle.

BUBBIE: Andrew will take care of it.

ME: Did you like it?

LILY: It's spicy. Like really spicy. It made my face feel hot. Do *you* like it?

I had never tried it but I told her Sweat was my favorite drink. She said hers too. I told her I could get her a discount on a case. She asked how. I said if you come up to my room I'll give you a promo code and you can order it. She said she was all over that. Bubbie Libby asked me to get her another beer and then told us to have fun.

I forgot that I had laid the Trendemic clothes out on my bed. She started holding everything up to her like she liked it.

ME: I bet this style would look good on you.

Feeling = Dirty and sneaky and disgusting and desperate for money. Is this how Gardner always feels?

LILY: Seriously?

ME: Totally hot. I can get you a deal if you want.

Feeling = I needed to wash my mouth out with Animaul body wash.

Lily was so excited she opened a PayPal account right there. She ordered the spray-painted jeans, a case of Sweat, the polka-dot turtleneck, and the denim jacket with the studs. I felt guilty because they were mostly boy clothes, so I gave her my Heart-breaker shirt for free. She liked it so much she literally hugged me.

Feeling = I will never understand girls.

— LATER

Lily

Friday, October 5, 2012

- Crushed Mountain Dew can.
- Glow-in-the-dark Frisbee.
- Mud-covered Nike Air Max basketball shoes
  with the swooshes covered in silver duct
  tape.
- Reusable water bottle in blue.
- Three used sparklers.
- Nerf water pistol.
- Purple-stained Popsicle stick.
- Basketball.
- Dollar bill L 89751377 D.

- Adidas Roundhouse basketball shoes.*
  Color: Aluminum. Logos covered in duct
  tape.
- Heartbreaker shirt.*

*I added two new things to my collection. Four if you count Duffy's nameless Maltese puppies. Who, by the way, keep scratching my closet door. They must be picking up the scent of Duffy's things. Ha! If anyone ever read that last sentence they'd swear I was a serial killer.

Thanks to Bubbie Libby's biannual trip to the bank, where she deposited six Social Security checks, I have been promoted from dog walker to dog sitter. This means I pick up the dogs after school and keep them until dinner. That's $35/week. If I hadn't spent most of my computer money on clothes, I'd be one semester away from typing on a crisp new Apple, instead of the rotten one I've had for years.

Unfortunately I have $86.27. Total. That's right. I have murdered my life's savings. The ironic part? I finally have a life.

Vanessa gets most of the credit for giving me such great advice. All remaining credit, however, goes to me for taking said advice and executing it. I have had success with pointers #1–4 (Be friendly, Stay under the radar, Be a good listener, Don't be a know-it-all) but #5 has been the real game changer. More on that in a minute. The rotten Apple has rebooted. Back to my British Identity and Literature paper.

Rebooting.

Pointer #5: Dress like the people you are trying to befriend. Eat the same foods. Drink the same drinks. The following chart details the times I have done that and the great success that ensued.

EXECUTED #5	GREAT SUCCESS
Drank Sweat at Duffy's house. It went down like liquid fire. Felt like a fever, looked like a sunburn. I said I loved it.	Duffy invited me to his room. He gave me his secret discount code. This shows he's starting to trust me.
Saw piles of avant-garde on Duffy's bed. I said polka dots and studs are totally my thing.	Spent one hour online-shopping with Duffy. He smelled salty from sweat. I smelled spicy like Sweat. He was the chips to my salsa.
Wore spray-painted jeans and Heartbreaker shirt to school.	Was invited to join the style club. They had a Preppy, a Goth, a Label Lover, a DIY, a Romantic, a Boho, a Diva, a Sporty, a Vintage, a Rocker, a Tease, a Grunge, and a Gaga. They were short a European and a Skater. Not anymore.

In addition, I received six compliments from Pubs. That Sheridan girl said I am doing a great job channeling Bryanboy. Compliment or insult? I Googled immediately. Born Bryan Grey Yambao, "Bryanboy" is a male fashion blogger from the Philippines with over 200,000 followers. A compliment indeed.

Wait, it gets better. Duffy introduced me to his friends Hud and Coops as "the biggest contributor to his charity." But the very best part? Duffy talks to me at school. Duffy talks to me at home. Today he called me Lil.

Naturally my parents had some inquiries. The Lily they raised doesn't wear spray-painted denim and studded jackets. So naturally, they wanted to know where I got the money and—more importantly—when my wardrobe became so "sui generis." They asked whom I was hanging out with and if Blake's style had been "compromised" too. A "Say No to Drugs" lecture was gathering strength. From there, it would spiral into a tornado of parental anxiety set to blow me back to Homie-land. Weathering the storm meant locking their fears in the storm cellar. It meant I had to lie.

~~~~~

Rebooting.

"Guess what, Mom? I was asked to join the prestigious Noble High style club. High Style, for short."

"What's so high style about a shirt stained with fake blood?"

"Look past the shirt. Focus on what the shirt represents."

"Slaughter?"

(Sigh.) "Maybe I'm explaining it wrong. Forget fashion. If you're thinking fashion it's no wonder you're confused. Think politics. Think *style* of politics."

"I don't know what to think." She winced, like I was a bad smell.

"This shirt speaks to the need for child labor laws in third world countries."

"And what do those jeans say? I ran out of canvas?"

"They're a nod to the graffiti movement in New York City, circa 1972."

"More like an affront."

"Graffiti is how inner-city kids express themselves. It's protest and politics through art. That's what High Style is. It's not about *who* we're wearing. It's about *why* we're wearing. Get it?"

"And who's paying for these...highly artistic expressions?"

"That's the best part." I smiled.

"It is?"

"Yep."

"Yes, not yep."

"Yes."

"Well," she said.

"We make the clothes ourselves."

"Explains the fit."

"Huh?"

"Pardon me."

"Pardon me?"

"Lily, you have to admit, they have a certain masculine edge, don't you think?"

"*Exactly!* I knew you'd get it. Typically protestors are male. Now you know why I'm so excited for our exploration of the women's movement."

"When is that?"

"Spring. Once the weather warms up. Because of the skirts and all."

"I completely understand," she said, the furrow between her brows suggesting otherwise.

~~~~~

Rebooting.

Vanessa wondered what inspired my new "look." She said people were talking about me and asked what happened to "staying under the radar." I told her they talked about me just as much when I wore my sweats. At least now it's good stuff. To which she replied, "True."

Blake, however, was harder to convince.

"Did you lose a bet?"

"No."

"Your mind?"

"No!"

"Join a circus?"

"No."

"A band?"

"No."

"A busker troupe?"

"Stop! I'm just experimenting."

"With Lady Gaga's rejects?"

"Better than the Wright brothers."

"Better than the Wrong brothers."

"Better than the Coxsackie sisters."

I used banter to evade Blake's questions. It worked for an entire week. Yesterday I broke.

He came over after school to "ride" the dogs. We stood on our boards, held the leashes, and let them run. It felt like water-skiing. We were having so much fun he actually dropped the subject of my clothes until I put on the mirrored aviator sunglasses I bought from Duffy. I had no idea LUV U, I C U, and HOT 4 U flashed across the lenses until Blake cracked up. He was laughing so hard he smashed into a parked car.

"Okay, what's his name?" he asked, sitting on the curb. A nameless dog jumped on his lap. He rubbed its ears. He kissed its nose. And then, "Oh. My. God!"

He knew.

I buried my face inside my studded jacket. Looking at Blake was like staring truth in the eye. I rarely liked what it reflected back.

"Andrew *Duffy*?"

My insides lurched at the sound of his name.

"The basketball guy?"

"Stop."

"That's why you've been dressing like Snooki?"

"Maybe," I squeaked.

"He *is* cute," Blake admitted. "I just pictured you with someone more—"

"Intellectual? Fringe? Dot gov?"

"Yeah."

"Makes sense."

"It does?"

"Sure. I pictured you with someone rational and friendly. And you're with Trike."

"Mike."

"Psych."

A Maltese licked the back of my hand.

"I can see why you like him, though," Blake said, leaning back on his elbows. "He's . . . different."

I clarified. "He's different because he's normal."

"Which is different for us."

"Exactly."

"I get it."

"I know."

~~~~~~

On the way back Blake asked if Duffy liked me too.

"I can't tell."

"Has he tried anything?"

"Blake!" The thought of kissing Duffy terrified me. The ratio of *things that could go well* to *things that could embarrass me for life* was 1:1,000,000,000,000,000,000,000,000,000.

"Has he texted or asked to hang or anything?"

"No. He invites me over to shop."

"Ha! That old excuse." Blake held the nameless dog's leash with one hand and tipped his paperboy cap with the other, proof that he subscribed to the I-shop-for-love channel.

"You think it means something?" I asked, jumping a crack in the road.

"Of course it does."

"What?"

"It means he's using clothes as an excuse to hang out. Guys are shy. They need a way in. Shopping is his way in."

"You think?"

"Um, Snooki, have you seen *my* wardrobe?"

"Yes, Amelia. I have."

~~~~~

When we got back Duffy was shooting hoops on his driveway. Blake hugged me goodbye, whispered "get some," and rolled on outta there. I would have killed him if I didn't love him so much.

"Back with the dogs," I announced.

"Interesting technique," he said as they pulled me up his driveway.

I giggled because I didn't know what to say.

Duffy shot a basket. "That your boyfriend?"

My heart bounced higher than the ball. I couldn't believe he asked me that.

"'S okay if you don't want to tell me," he said, shooting again.

(Swish.)

"Tell you *what*?"

"If that guy is your boyfriend."

I needed Vanessa or Blake or anyone who might know what I should do next. If I said yes, would that make him jealous? Would jealousy make him like me more? Or give up and move on? If I said Blake wasn't my boyfriend, he'd think I was incapable of being liked. Or that I liked Blake but he didn't like—

"I'm getting a new box of clothes tomorrow," he said. "If you want to come by."

"Blake is gay."

Lily Bader-Huffman-Dead

Sheridan

10.5.12

INT. LAVENDER BATH—NIGHT.

SHERIDAN puts quill to paper while soaking in the memories of her first date earlier that evening.

Logan pulled up to my house and honked. I kissed my parents goodbye and told them to put the camera down. This wasn't a date. They weren't missing any big moments. I was simply getting a ride to rehearsal with a friend. Dad said he wasn't questioning my plan, only my motive. I dug through my purse to hide the fact that his *CSI* jargon was freaking me out. Did he know I was about to commit a crime?

Mom tried to explain.

Your father isn't questioning the fact that you're going to rehearsal with this boy—

Logan.

Logan. It's just that he, we, think you've spent a long time getting ready.

So?

So maybe Logan means more to you than—

Than what, Mom? A ride? Because that's all he is. A ride. I spent a long time getting ready because I am trying to get into character.

But you're the—

It's okay. You can say understudy. But I'm also a professional. I need to be ready in case Octavia gets taken out by a truck or something.

Sheridan! (Them.)

Excuse me for being optimistic.

Another honk.

Gotta go.

I bolted.

Logan said *wow* when he saw me. I knew Scarlett Johansson was the right call for a date. Rubenesque undercarriage, sexy, and daring; I needed to be all of those things. And I was.

My hair was sculpted to the side and loosely curled at the bottom. Like Scarlett I played up my lips with berry-colored gloss ("Maybe she's born with it") while downplaying the eyes with mascara and gold shadow. I stuffed my pear parts into skinny jeans and showcased my flat midriff with a boxy tank that "accidentally" shot north when I moved. And my pointy faux snakeskin pumps? Sssssssssssssexy.

The "daring" is everything that happened next.

The dealership was closed when we got there. Floppy Beemer was our only witness. I made Logan turn around while I disabled the alarm system, then made him triple swear he'd never talk about this.

Dude, this is so hot.

I wanted to turn around and run. Not because I was afraid of getting busted. But because Logan was rubbing his hands together really quickly and licking his lips. Like he was about to eat a giant steak and I was the side of potatoes. If I was going to be anyone's side I didn't want to be his. But that was Sheridan talking and this night belonged to Scarlett.

I lifted the keys from the case and jangled them in front of Logan's eyes the way he had done to Audri back on the first day of school. The memory gave me a chill. It was hard to believe that was only a few weeks ago. My life has changed so much since then. Audri, the play, this crime. None of it seemed possible. And yet, here I was. Helping some Biff drive Dad's prized possession.

Let's do this! Logan snatched the keys from my hand, unlocked the door, and tossed his suede jacket into the backseat. I laughed when he slipped on fingerless driving gloves and said, *M3 GTR ready for liftoff.*

I thought he was joking. He wasn't. The guy blasted out of the dealership before my seat belt clicked, and shot down Old Bell Road doing 90. The speed limit is 35.

Slow down!

I can't! My shoe is stuck on the gas!

This time he was joking but I didn't laugh. I squeezed his arm. *Seriously! Slow down.*

Drivers flashed their headlights. Pedestrians scurried.

Logan, please! Someone is gonna call the cops.

What are they gonna call them? Pigs? (Him, not being funny.)

Drop to 60!

He took it to 100. I blamed Octavia. She drove me to this. (PUN INTENDED!)

Deer!

Where? Logan stomped on the brake. We flew forward. *Incredible control.*

He sat there gripping the wheel, staring out at the road ahead. He was practically panting. *I don't see any deer.*

My text alert chirped. I leaned forward to get my purse off the floor. Logan jammed the gas. My head slammed back against the seat.

I felt dizzy. Clammy. Heavy. Achy. I found my phone. Audri. She just asked Jagger to Octavia's party. He said yes.

Yay! (Me texting.)

My intestines began to throb. I started to feel sick. I can't remember if it was Logan's driving, the texting while speeding, or not being invited to their party that did it. All I remember is that Scarlett was gone and Sheridan was back.

Guess I wasn't invited. (I texted.)

I told O to put you on the list. She promised. Maybe it's in your junk mail.

I rolled down the window.

Sher, you believe me, right?

I wanted to type *yes*, but we were about to break the sound barrier and my mouth was starting to water. Then came the prickly sweat.

I stuck my head out the window. My hair uncoiffed and blew into my gloss. Logan was clueless. To him the open windows were an opportunity to poke himself out the moon roof and drive with his knees. The car began to sway. I tugged on his Diesels.

Sit down!

Whooooo-hooooooooooooo!

I began to taste batteries. I felt around the backseat for Logan's jacket.

He was howling out the moon roof and didn't hear my yeti burp. Or the splat of puke that pooled in the satin lining of his Hugo Boss bomber. Or me whipping the suede barf bag onto Old Bell Road. The screeching tires drowned everything out.

We made it back to the dealership without an arrest, a hit-and-run, or death. Logan said he was so excited he could kiss me.

I didn't want anything of the sort. And not just because I had puke breath. After that ride, after what I risked for him, I hated him even more than Octavia. I invited him to Octavia's party.

He accepted without hesitation.

We spent the next hour searching the dealership for his

jacket. He said it was really expensive. He just got it. It was his favorite. His house keys were in there.

I acted like someone who cared. It was quite the performance. Where are the cameras when you need them?

To Be Continued...

END SCENE.

Jagger

Oct. 5.

I took one of Randy's Chihuahua puppies for a late-night walk.
The tan one. I was smiling too much to be alone.

Audri invited me to a party.

As her date.

A BMW zoomed by.

The pup started to shake.

I found a suede coat on Old Bell Road.

The label said Hugo Boss.

Lucky day!

I'd wrap the shaking dog in the coat. I'd wear it to the party
with Audri. I'd sell it after and use the money to buy her
flowers.

I picked it up.

It was filled with puke so I dropped it.

I still felt lucky.

-J

Duffy

Monday

Feeling = Unlucky.

My striped sweatbands are missing. This day is going to suck.

Later.

Feeling = Knew it.

We had one hour and forty-five minutes to kill before practice. The guys wanted pizza. I said go without me. I wanted to run home and find my sweatbands. Also, I can't afford pizza. Not that they would have believed me. Every day I show up wearing a slick watch or belt. I have new headphones, a tablet, and a "text book" that lets me send messages in class without getting caught. Rumors are going around that I'm endorsed and raking it in. The *Noble High Times* nicknamed me Golden Boy because of my shoes. They "applaud my philanthropic spirit" (whatever that means). They suspect I am "singlehandedly supporting the entire cause" because I "rarely ask for donations and have yet to reveal the charity's name."

Mandy lost it when she read that. Then she made me recycle as many copies as I could find so Mom and Dad wouldn't see it.

Hud and Coops have been begging me to come clean. They know something is up and keep asking if that Lily girl is involved because we're so style-y all of a sudden and she's always staring at me. I've been saying they're crazy. But that's not going to fly anymore. Not after they saw the slick Hummer parked at the Pick and Flick.

Everyone was standing around like Jay-Z was inside. There was a sign in the window with my name on it. I thought it was a joke.

COOPS: Have fun at *home*, Golden Boy.

ME: Huh?

HUD: Yeah guys, nothing is going on. We must be *crazy*.

A few of them laughed.

HUD: See ya, Slick. We'll be at Domino's if you need us. Just look for the poor dudes.

COOPS: With the gold shoes.

LOGO: I can't believe you girls paid for those things.

ME: Guys, I have no clue what this is about. Seriously!

They walked away laughing.

I was going to chase after them when Anton rolled down a tinted window and told me to get in.

He was wearing a black leather jumpsuit. It crackled when he crossed his legs.

ANTON: Cappuccino? The bean has been harvested with the a-sa-yeeee berry.

ME: No, thanks.

He took a sip from a tiny mug. The way he held out his pinky reminded me of Amelia and Mandy playing tea party. Only his was sprayed orange and covered in hair.

The Hummer pulled away from the curb.

ME: Where are we going?

We drove past the guys. Hud and Coops acted like they didn't notice.

Feeling = Like I swallowed a sock.

ANTON: Don't you read *anything*?

Feeling = No.

ANTON: Your itinerary was in the last box.

I remember seeing something. But Lily was over and she said she was in a buying mood so I got right to the selling. Then *Adventure Time* was on.

ME: I didn't see anything.

Anton puckered and took another sip.

ME: Anton, I have practice in—

ANTON: I'll have you back in twenty minutes. I just want you to see the venue.

Feeling = What's a venue?

We pulled up to a warehouse. I started to panic. Was this about my debt? Was I about to get whacked? I reached for the door handle. It was locked.

ME: What's happening? Why are we here?

ANTON: I'm going to kill you.

I didn't yawn but I went deaf anyway. I thought about my grieving parents. They would blame themselves.

ME: But my sales are good. I'll just need a few more—

ANTON: Relax. I'm kidding. Come. Let's see the catwalk.

Turns out I am contracted to co-host a fashion show Friday night. Each It Guy has to fill twenty seats. They should go to top clients only. Everything the models wear will be sold at the after-party. High-end brands only. I have the potential to pay off the rest of my debt in this one night.

I didn't tell Anton my "top clients" were Lily, the next-door neighbor. I just said, "Cool."

Feeling = Four days to find nineteen top clients.

Anton dropped me back at school but I was late for practice. Everyone was on the bleachers. No one said hi or looked at me or hazed me for reeking like Anton's Animaul cologne. The coach didn't make me do sprints. It's like I wasn't there.

I sat to the left of Hud. He slid to the right.

ME: Really? So it's like that?

HUD: You gonna tell me where you were?

ME: It was nothing.

HUD: Then yeah, it's like that.

The coach pulled a piece of paper out of a wool beanie.

COACH: Number ten.

LOGO: Yes!

Feeling = What's going on?

I had to piece it all together because no one would talk to me.

Rumson was down one player so we had to lose one too. The younger guys volunteered because Octavia is having a party and they wanted to go. Bammer drew numbers. Logo won. He already has a date. Some "wild" freshman. He's pumped to sit this one out.

We start playing a scrimmage and I'm trying to really focus, which is not easy since everyone is either ignoring me or calling me Slick. I shoot a basket. No one high-fives me. I can't wait to pay off my debt and be done with this whole thing. I shoot another basket. No one says a thing. I can't wait for life to get back to normal. Four more days and I should be done. Four more days until Friday. Four more days until normal. Four more days until—I lost the ball. Realizing the Rumson game is the same night as your fashion show will do that to a guy.

I have to get out of that game.

I shoot another basket.

The coach will never let me off the hook. Rumson is too good. I score too much. Logo will never give me his pass. I can't tell anyone the truth. I shoot another basket. I have to think of something. I do. I steal the ball from Ryan. Greg is clear. He tells me to pass. I don't. I line up the shot. I know I should pass. I don't. I jump. I throw. I land. I Wipe. Problem solved.

I land on my shin but say it's my ankle. I'm not hurt but moan like I am. I limp off. Hud and Coops don't ask if I'm okay. They know I am. They know I did it on purpose. But they don't ask why. They don't seem to care.

I tell Coach Bammer I can't play Rumson on Friday. He is bummed. He was counting on me to crush them.

Logo has to play now and will miss the party. He thinks I did this on purpose. Hud and Coops know I did. They know it has to do with my slick new lifestyle.

Feeling = How am I going to find nineteen people on Friday when no one is talking to me?

— LATER

Sheridan

10.9.12

INT. NOBLE HIGH—AFTERNOON.

Logan is a total ass for not telling me he has a basketball game Friday night. Especially since I didn't find out from him. Octavia told me.

Actually, she told Audri. I was listening again. We were leaving rehearsal and she was talking about changing the party to Saturday night instead of Friday.

Why? (Audri.)

Logan has a game Friday night. (Octavia.)

No, he doesn't. (Me.)

Oh, where did you come from? (Octavia, pretending she didn't see me, as usual.)

What do you mean he doesn't have a game Friday? (Audri.) *Why would he lie?*

Yeah, why would he lie? (Octavia.)

No idea. But he doesn't have a game. (Me, only super confident.)

Octavia stopped and turned to face me. Her summer tan had faded. She looked less Kardashian and more Hilton.

How do you know what Logan is doing Friday night? (Octavia.)

Audri had no clue what I was about to say. I had purposely not told her I asked Logan to the party. I didn't want her to feel in the middle of all this. Mature of me, right? I know.

Octavia tapped her glitter Converse. I told her how I knew.

What do you mean you're taking him to my party? (Octavia.) *I didn't even invite you.*

I shot Audri a look. It ricocheted off her glasses and hit Octavia.

O, you said she was on the list. (Audri.) *You promised.*

I was talking about a different list. (Octavia.)

Octavia! (Audri.)

It doesn't matter. Logan and I can do something else that night. (Me.)

Like go to Rumson and watch his game. (Octavia.)

He. Doesn't. Haveagame! (Me.)

Octavia opened the door of the gym and shouted: *Do you guys have a game Friday night?*

A few of the guys shouted back. One of them was Logan. They all said yes. She let the door slam shut. *You were saying.*

Line! Can I get a line? I had no idea how to play it. Octavia had won. She always won.

A sudden bang made us jump. A cute junior had just kicked in his locker. Principal Alden called after him. His name was A.J. Principal Alden told him to stop. A.J. ran. When Octavia's head was turned I ran too. Down the hall, around the corner, past the lockers and—*oof!*

I tripped on a cane.

I landed like a cat, on all fours. My book bag spilled open. A FemFresh rolled out and stopped in the middle of the floor. Jagger the Orphan saw it and walked the other way. Like it had teeth or something.

It's just a tampon! (Me.)

Jagger walked faster.

Duffy put it back in my bag.

You're not scared of it? (Me.)

Two older sisters, remember? (Duffy.)

My knee throbbed.

My cane slipped when I shut my locker. (Duffy.) *You okay?*

I didn't want to make him feel bad so I said I was.

What happened to you?

Basketball. (Duffy.)

I'm starting to hate that sport. (Me.)

Why?

More like a player. (Me.)

It was an accident. I swear.

Not you. I giggled. *Logan.*

You mean Logo? Bet I hate him more.

I do.

No, I do.

No, me.

Me.

We left school together. After three blocks of Logan-loathing we talked about best friends—how they change or move on, and how that hurts. After a while Duffy stopped limping. I didn't, so he gave me his cane.

He walked all the way to my house. The M3 GTR was parked in the driveway. I waited for him to go all crazy and start humping it. He didn't. I liked that. He asked what I was doing Friday night. I said nothing. He asked if I wanted to go to a fashion show. I thought he was joking until he said he wasn't. He told me I could bring as many friends as I wanted. It wasn't a date. But it was something. And I had nothing. So I said yes.

To Be Continued...

END SCENE.

Jagger

Sheridan Spencer knows.

-J

Vanessa

October 10th

Mom and Dad had a huge blowout Sunday night. I don't know how it started but I heard how it ended. The entire neighborhood did.

Mom said married couples have affairs at the hotel all the time. There was a time when she couldn't understand that kind of betrayal—cheating on someone you love. But she understands it now. Because people need affection to survive. Affection fuels the heart. If we can't get it from our partners we look for it somewhere else.

Dad told her to stop being so dramatic. And that he says he loves her all the time. She said talk is cheap. I don't want to hear it, I want to *feel* it. He asked if it was that time of the month.

She said, "Yes, what's your excuse?"

Then she threw a bunch of clothes in a wheelie and said she'd be spending the night at the hotel. He wished her luck with the affair and went back to the computer.

Mom called that night to tell me and A.J. she loves us. I cried and asked when she was coming home. She said she was working late and she'd see me in the morning.

It's Wednesday. She's still not back.

I keep begging Dad to make her come home. He says he can't make that woman do anything and she'll come when she's ready.

We needed Beni's.

But I had just gotten another B and my bracelets were being held by U.S. Customs officials. The mindless bureaucrats who kept putting me on hold, transferring me, and disconnecting my calls said they don't know why. They don't know when I will have them. I asked if they knew anything, like how unequivocally stupid they are. They hung up.

The Girl Scouts Young Women of Distinction contest is in two weeks. Without my SWAPs I can't enter. Without entering I can't win. I am still not captain of the track team. Principal Alden is not easily impressed. Debate club was a bust. And the Phoenix Five thing is months away. The future of our family and the outer layer of my epidermis rested on A.J.'s rounded shoulders.[46]

I sat on the roof and waited for him to get home from work.

....

[46] I can't believe I just wrote that. I can't believe it's true.

I prayed he sold a car. If he didn't I prayed he'd lie and say he did.

Then we got a call from the school. A.J. kicked in a locker and took off. Dad tried to reach him at work. Mr. Spencer said he fired A.J. that afternoon. He stole the M3 GTR and took it for a joy ride. Dad asked if he was sure. A.J. loved this job and wouldn't have done anything to jeopardize it. But we all knew he loved that car even more so we weren't surprised.

When A.J. got home Dad lost it. I ran up to the roof, blasted my iTouch, and cried.[47]

How could I have been so unequivocally selfish?[48] Those grades were what held my family together. And I let them slip for a boy. A boy who hasn't even asked me out even though he says things like, "I love this girl."

I listened to that Adele song "Someone Like You" and cried holes through my emotional ozone layer.[49] I mean, do you know how hard it is to get straight A's and win awards and wear long sleeves in the summer? It's an endless marathon of exhausting.

I knew A.J. would mess this up but I let myself believe he

---

[47] I know there are Haitian orphans and even some local ones who have it a lot worse than me. Which only made me feel worse than ever.

[48] Writing "unequivocally" makes me feel unequivocally smart.

[49] "Emotional Ozone"—good name for a poem!

wouldn't.[50] Not because I had faith in him. More because I needed a rest.

I listened to the Adele song again and imagined playing it for Blake. That's when A.J. showed up on the roof and sat beside me. He hung his head between his knees. It was his turn to cry.

"I didn't do it, Ness."

"Why do they think you did?"

"Because I love that car. I'm the new guy. I'm in high school. I dunno."

"Well, what did they say?"

"Just that someone added twenty miles to it Friday night."

"That doesn't prove anything."

A.J. gazed past the satellite dishes and phone wires and sighed. "They found a Noble High key chain on the backseat."

"Oh."

His blue eyes filled again. I rested my hand on his back. He was wearing his favorite flannel—purple-and-gray plaid. The colors were not as vibrant as they used to be. None of us were.

"Wait," I said, breaking the silence. "You have a Noble High key ring?"

"Oh, sure," he said. "I just love how it matches my Noble High sweats and my Noble High hat and my Noble High binders."

....

[50] Mom says feelings are more reliable than thoughts. I should have listened.

"So, it wasn't you."

"I told you that."

We didn't speak again for a while. I was thinking about life and how unfair it can be. Then A.J. said, "You think Mom and Dad will get divorced?"

"I don't know."

"How are your grades?"

"Crap," I said.

Nothing about that was funny but we smiled anyway.

"Without your A's and my job, how are we going to fix this?" he asked.

We never talked openly about Beni's or why we loved it so much. I convinced myself that A.J. liked going for the food. Because if A.J. went for the peace, like I did, then A.J. knew about the dysfunction. And if he knew about the dysfunction it had to be real. I couldn't wave it away like a lone wisp of dandelion fluff. I'd have to admit that the fluff was part of something bigger. A beanstalk I didn't want to see.

"You went to stop the fighting too?"

"No, the teppanyaki. That high-speed chopping never gets old," he said. "Jeez, does everyone in this family think I'm a moron?"

"Kind of," I said.

"Okay, genius, now what?"

Midterms were coming out this Monday and I didn't have a single A. I knew with a little effort—okay, a lot—I could get my grades up and we'd be back on track. But we didn't have time for that; Mom was gone now.

"How badly do you want this?" I asked.

"Uh, I don't want Mom and Dad to get divorced, if that's what you're asking."

"So you'd do anything to save their marriage?"

"'Course," A.J. said.

I paused to assess the desperation behind his eyes.

"Anything?"

"Yes!"

"Teach me how to hack."

> *Whatever relationships you have attracted in your life at this moment, are precisely the ones you need in your life at this moment.*

> —Deepak Chopra

Lily

Wednesday, October 10, 2012

The buttery aroma of béchamel sauce welcomed me home from school. I hadn't even pulled my key out of the door when Mom shouted, "Lily, in the kitchen. Now!"

I wondered if she busted the lock on my journal. If she had, Karb, Kalorie, and Kardio were the least of my concerns. She'd know about my Duffy obsession, that my savings is now an homage to Bryanboy, that I toss my Hebrew National salami because it has Dead Sea amounts of sodium. Most of all, she'd know how badly I long for normal. A longing that negates everything she's ever taught me.

Anyway, it was a false alarm. I was late for International Cuisine Night and she was koncerned (ha!).

ICN is Mom's way of filling my free time with activities I would never tell a Pub person—living or dead—about. Ever. The point is for me to translate a foreign recipe, cook it, serve it, and digest it. You can see why I wasn't racing home.

"Sorry, Mom, I had a style club meeting," I said, peering into the bubbling saucepot. "What are you making?"

"What *you* were supposed to be making," she snipped. "Kosher Croque Tartiflette."

"Oy, how French."

She wiped her hands on a black dishcloth and tossed it on the island. "Lily, should I be concerned?"

"About what?"

"Look at you."

Concern would not be an uncommon reaction to the bike chain suspenders that held up my striped golf pants. But they were a small price to pay for Pub-ularity.

"Bubbie Libby from next door stopped by," she continued. "You were supposed to walk . . ."

"It's okay, they don't have names."

"You didn't even call her. That's not like you. You're more responsible than that. . . ." Her voice trailed off. "You used to be."

"What's that supposed to mean?"

"It means I haven't seen a single grade since that A you got in Algebra."

"A-plus."

"Still."

"Mom, I'm fine. I promise. I was at school. That's all."

"Not for long," she mumbled.

"Huh?"

"Pardon me."

"Sorry. Pardon me?"

"I was reminding you of our agreement. Straight A's or you're back at home."

The preheat alert beeped. She put in the Croque and let the oven door slam shut.

"Mmmmm, what's that smell? *Très magnifique*," Dad said, home from work. He stuffed his commuter train newspapers in the recycle bin, kissed us hello, and asked again what smelled so good. We didn't answer. Mom turned her back to me and sighed. I rolled my eyes.

"Looks like everything is under control in here." He poured a glass of red wine and hurried off. "Call me when it's ready."

Dad is a senior editor at the *New York Times*. He is the most intelligent person I have ever met. He manages a department of smart journalists because he's even smarter than they are. But the guy is seriously challenged when it comes to girl fights.

After he left, Mom said, "I'm not kidding, Lily. I will pull you out of that school tomorrow if I have to."

When I was three, I put a dry cleaning bag over my face and tried to breathe because my mom said not to. I wasn't getting any air so I breathed harder. That made it worse. My lungs became bricks and my face turned blue. Leaving Noble and going back to Homie would feel more stifling.

"Am I clear?"

"Yeah, I get it."

"Yes, I understand."

UGH!

"Yes, I understand."

I understood that I couldn't leave Blake, Vanessa, or Duffy. I wasn't exactly mentally stimulated by the girls in style club, but I had fun looking through celebrity magazines and debating who wore it best. The point is, I am learning to function in society. To live among my peers. To connect. Of the plethora of things Mom taught me, she never taught that. She refused.

While the Croque cooked, I thought about my bungee-ing grades (A+, B+, B, A-, B, A, C). Correction. Okay, that's a lie. I should have. Instead, I stared at the side of Duffy's house and wondered why he left school with Sheridan yesterday. What they talked about. Why we never walked home together. If he got the Evite to Octavia's girl-ask-boy party Friday night. If it was his first house party too. What he would wear. What he thought I should wear. If Octavia's parents were going to be there. If not, what he would tell his parents. What he thought I should tell mine. What he would say if I asked him to be my date.

I had to know. Then I'd focus on my bungee-ing grades.

"Mom, how long until dinner?"

"Five minutes."

"I'm going to apologize to Bubbie Libby," I said. "Be right back."

When Duffy's sister Mandy opened the door, the dogs made a break straight for my house.

"Not today, girls," I called. "Come back!"

They ignored me so I chased after them. "It would be so much easier if they had names!"

"What do you think of Violet and Seraphina?" Mandy asked as I dumped them back in the foyer.

"Ben Affleck and Jennifer Garner's daughters?"

She hugged me. Mandy Duffy of the 3Ms hugged me. "Ha! I can't believe you got that. No one here knows what I'm talking about."

I wanted to skate down the street shouting: I got it! I was right! Move over French, Spanish, and Hebrew! I speak the international language of pop culture now! Thank you, Noble! Thank you, style club! Thank you, *Us Weekly*! Thank you alllllll!

"Duff! There's a hottie here to see you!" Mandy called, accepting me as one of her own.

I should have corrected her. I should have told her I was there to see Bubbie Libby. But I didn't. Because I wasn't.

Duffy came charging down the stairs and all I could think was, *Uh-oh*. And then, *What am I doing? A girl like me can't ask a guy like this to a Pub party. Bad idea, Lily! Go ask someone your own size. You're not tall enough for this roller coaster. Ask Blake....*

"Oh," Duffy said, disappointed. "Hey, Lily."

"Expecting someone else?"

He opened his mouth to answer but I cut him off. "What are you doing Friday night?"

"O-kayyy," Mandy said, backing away from an imaginary gun.

"Sorry," I said, blushing. And then, "Hey, your ankle is better."

"Oh, uh, not really, I, uh, I let it breathe at night. The doctor says to keep it wrapped for another few days, though, so . . ."

"Oh."

"Actually," he said, "I'm glad you're here."

"Really, why?"

"You're in style club, right?"

"Yeah."

"How many girls are in that?"

"Fifteen?" I said. It came out sounding more like a question.

"Cool." He stuffed his hands in the pocket of his hoodie. Was he nervous too? "Uh . . . you think you'd . . . all be into going to a—"

"Want to go to Octavia's party?" I blurted. Flattering as his nervousness was, I couldn't stand to watch him suffer.

"—fashion show Friday night?"

"Fashion show?"

He snickered. He couldn't believe it either. "Yeah."

"What about Octavia's party?"

"This is gonna be slick. And since your club is all about style, I figured—"

"Okay. What time will you be picking me up?" I laughed because we live next door and I know he doesn't drive.

"I have to go early. Can we meet there?"

"Sure."

"Cool. Oh, and bring Blake if you want. You know, cuz he might be into it."

251

What he probably wanted to say was, "I know Blake is gay and won't be a threat so if it makes you more comfortable to have him tag along, go for it." But he was being discreet and I appreciated that. So I winked to let him know we were on the same page. I must have been radiating extreme love-heat because Duffy's cheeks got red.

"Oh, uh, hold on...."

He ran upstairs and returned with a stack of flyers. "These will get everyone in."

I took them and ran home. I would have run around the planet if dinner wasn't ready. I had that much joy to burn. I couldn't wait to tell Blake everything. Except the part about how he was invited. Because I, Lily Bader-Huffman-Duffy, am tall enough for this roller coaster. And I'm ready to ride it alone....

Then I'll study.

Lily Bader-Huffman-Duffy

Lily Bader-Huffman-Duffy

Lily Bader-Huffman-Duffy

Lily Bader-Huffman-Duffy

Lily Bader-Huffman-Duffy

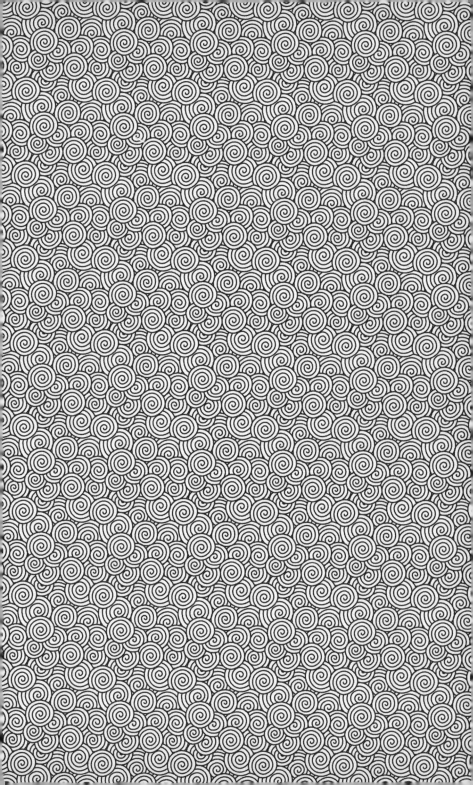

Vanessa

October 10th

Forgive me, Journal, for I have sinned.

Instead of asking "What's the problem?" ask
"What's the creative opportunity?"

—Deepak Chopra

October 11th

Blake had a dentist appointment during lunch so Lily and I sat alone. She was asked to join the style club table and I am always fielding random invites, but she wanted to talk so I gave her my full attention.[51]

She opened by asking if I was okay. Apparently I looked tired and had been acting "jumpy." I scratched my arms and said I was fine. Then she pointed at my tray.[52] I told her I was

---

[51] Does she know what I did?

[52] Two napkins and a spoon.

on a juice cleanse and asked what the big news was. She said she has a date with Andrew Duffy.

I was relieved. Then shocked.

"Duffy?"

She smiled a huge smile. "Friday night."

"Really?"

She whipped her salami sandwich in the trash and said, "Why is that so hard to believe?"

"I just never pictured you two together. You're like..."

"What?"

"Different. Like oil and water. I can't picture you mixing."

"Who is the water?" she asked.

"You, of course. You're much smarter than him."

"It's smarter than *he*," she said.

I would have chucked a french fry at her if I had one. So I threw the napkin instead. She apologized for sounding like her mom.

"Being smart isn't everything, you know."

"You're only saying that because you're going to get straight A's on your midterm report."

"What midterm?"

"The one that comes out Monday."

"What? Are you sure?"

I told her I was. This freaked her out. Then Principal Alden walked into the cafeteria.

He stood at the door and looked around. I became unequivocally itchy. Did he know?

He looked right at me and did that two-finger wave that says *Hey you, yeah, you, look over here!* I pointed at my speeding heart. He nodded, *Yeah, you.* I stood while Lily was talking. I didn't care. I wanted to go peacefully. I didn't want a scene. But it was too late. He started making his way toward me. Everyone was staring.

My hands began shaking. Lily asked what was happening. My mouth was too dry to answer.

Principal Alden grabbed my elbow and guided me toward an empty corner.

"What's going on?"

He took off his glasses and looked right at me. "Vanessa, it's about your transcripts...."

And there it was. The life-flashing-before-you moment I assumed was just for soap opera characters. My parents' faces began flip-booking into different expressions of disappointment. Not much of a life, I know. But that's really what I saw.

"I reviewed your transcripts from middle school," Principal Alden said. "They were outstanding. You got straight A's on your midterm report...."

"Uh-huh..."

"Well, Vanessa, you strike me as a smart girl. One who makes good choices..."[53]

....

[53] His breath smelled like coffee.

"Yes, sir."

"So tell me..."

Ohnogodpleasenogodpleaseno...

"How did your brother turn out so...different?"

"Huh?"

"He was sent to my office again today. I left word with your parents but I was wondering if you could give me some insight. Is everything okay at home?"

I wanted to hug this Starbucks-scented man. I cried with relief instead.

"I knew it," he said, cupping my shoulder. "When you're around kids as long as I've been, you see the signs. Things are not okay. You tried to tell me that the other day and I shut you out. I'm sorry for that, Vanessa. But I am all ears now. Talk to me, Vanessa. It's safe. Would you like to go to my office?"

Tears of joy Niagara-ed down my cheeks. He had no clue what I did!

"It's my parents," I sniffled, suddenly grateful for their dysfunction. "They're kind of separated and it's been hard on us."

"How are you managing to stay so focused? I mean, straight A's?"

"School is my escape," I said, "and escaping is A.J.'s."[54]

He nodded like he was right there with me.

....

[54] Another great line. And yes, I'm bragging because I deserve to. I was under a ton of pressure when I came up with that.

"Sir?" I said, batting my Bambi lashes. "Our dad is great...
but..."

"Go on..."

"...But the separation has been hard on him too and he's
kind of lost...in his own world, you know?"

He nodded. "I do."

"A.J. could really use a father figure right now. Go easy on
him, if you can."

"Understood." He winked. "Oh, and Vanessa?"

"Yes?"

"Keep up the great work."

I smiled humbly.[55]

I flashed Lily a ginormous thumbs-up as I glided back to
our table.

"What was that all about?"

"A.J.'s messing up again."

She sighed. "I know the feeling."

She was picking her cuticles so, in spite of my desire to ask if
Blake had a date for Octavia's party, I thought it best to focus
on her. "What's wrong?"

She burst into tears. "I'm done."

"Ohmygod Lil, do you have a disease?"

This made her laugh so hard snot bubbled from her nose.
She grabbed my napkin and blew. "I have to leave Noble."

---

[55] Hello, Principal's Award.

259

"What? No! Why?"

I was just starting to trust Lily. Without her I'd feel lonely and alone.[56]

"I'm only allowed to be here if my grades stay as high as they were when I was a Homie. The second they fall I'm out. And they fell, big-time."

"Why did you agree to *that*?"

"I had no choice. It was the only way my mom would let me come." She started crying again. "And now midterms will be out and . . . what am I going to do?"

"Come," I said, grabbing her unsightly fake raccoon-pelt bag and leading her to the bathroom.

"My life is over."

"Shhhh, it's okay. It's not over."

"It is!"

"It's not!"

"It is!"

"It's NOT!"

"Vanessa, it is. Why do you keep saying it's not when it is?" Everyone in the hall was staring at us.

"Be. Cause," I insisted.

"Because whyyyy?"

"Because I have a solution."

---

[56] These words may seem redundant but they're not. They are two different things and I would feel them both.

"What kind of solution?"

"A good one."

When we got to the bathroom I told her.

The less you open your heart to others, the more your heart suffers.

—Deepak Chopra

Lily

Thursday, October 11, 2012

The barter system was used to exchange goods and services before the invention of money. It can be traced as far back as 6000 BC. There are roughly 192 different types of currency in circulation today, and yet the barter system can still be useful.

I will go light on the specifics for reasons I cannot disclose. Vanessa and I had a total heart-to-heart. I told her about my scholastic dilemma and she offered a solution (that's code for the thing I cannot disclose). I would never agree to something like that if my entire future didn't depend on it. But it does. So I did. I will say this: all parties benefited from the transaction. With one possible exception: Blake.

I offered to repay her in any way I possibly could.

She told me there was this one thing....

Turns out she had asked Blake to Octavia's party and he wouldn't commit. Her only request was for me to make him say yes. I told her I wasn't sure I could do that. She told me her "solution" was bigger than what she was asking from me. In barter-speak, I was getting a much better deal.

So I skated to Blake's house after school to settle an old debt.

"Remember what you said on September fifth?" I asked.

"That you have Coxsackie?"

His mouth was frozen from root canal, so it sounded more like "Cothakie."

"No, the other thing."

"That you needed to thave your piths?"

"No! That you owed me."

"For what?"

"For going to Noble with you."

He sat up on his bed. "Whath thith about?"

"I need you to say yes to Vanessa."

"Theriuthly?" He flopped back down as if hit by a dart. "Lily, I'm theeing thomeone."

"Just this one time. I swear. Then we'll be even. She really likes you, Blake, and you don't want me to tell her you're gay, so..."

"Can't you jutht thay I'm ethperienthing complicathions from root canal?"

"You said you'd do anything to pay me back. You did. I transcribed the entire conversation in my journal."

He held a bag of ice to his jaw. "Ithint thith going to lead her on even more?"

"Be dorky or something. Turn her off. Tell her you're gay. I don't care. Just please!"

"Why ith thith tho important?"

I swiped the pillow from behind his head and lay down beside him. "Can I trust you?"

He tossed the bag of ice at my face. "You're theriuthly asthing if you can trutht me?"

I told him everything. He texted Vanessa the moment I was done and accepted her invitation. She texted back a giant YAY.

Problem tholved.

Lily Bader-Huffman-Duffy

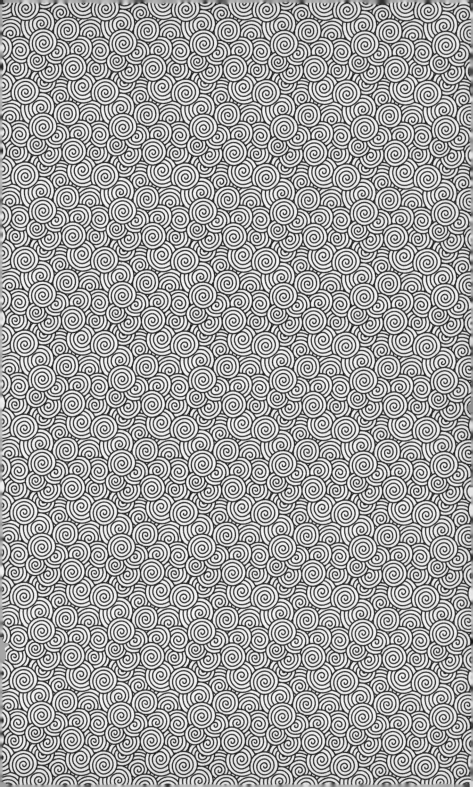

Sheridan

10.12.12

INT. HELL—NIGHT.

SHERIDAN zips up her favorite jeans and slips on a turquoise peasant top. Her hair is in a low pony and her lips are glossed nude. She checks her smile in the mirror and is pleased. She is pear-shaped and fabulous. Channels are for flat-screens, she decides. Tonight she will go to the fashion show as herself.

BIG MISTAKE #1!

This newfound confidence came from my walks with Duffy. After a few blocks I'd forget all about my channel du jour and accidentally slip back into me. Then he would stop limping or flip down his hood and we'd just...be.

You're like a sister-mutt. (Duffy.)

A what?

A sister-mutt. A mix of Amelia and Mandy.

(I laughed.) *Explain.*

Amelia is smart and cool but annoying. Mandy is pretty and funny but annoying. You're smart and cool and pretty and funny but not annoying. Like a mutt of my sisters.

O-kayyy. (Me, like someone who doesn't live to be told that kind of thing.) *And you're like a...a band-friend.*

Explain.

You're cute like the guys in One Direction without the annoying accent part. And you're easy to hang out with like my friend Audri without the annoying Octavia part. A band-friend.

I like that.

Did you ever say the word "annoying" over and over again? (Me.)

No.

Try it. (Me.)

Annoying. It sounds like a-nong.

A-nong, could be a city in Vietnam. (Me.)

We should send Logan to A-nong. (Duffy.)

By UPS. (Me.)

Ground. (Duffy.)

We had a lot of deep conversations like that. Where we looked at life in new ways that made me feel 5-hour ENERGY pumped. Which is why I decided to go to the fashion show as Sheridan Spencer. Because no other actress had been cast as a sister-mutt. And I wanted to stay with that for a while.

Mom and Dad left me at the warehouse with a stack of taxi vouchers in case Duffy couldn't give me a ride home. I also got a complete printout of their itinerary in case I needed to reach them. I told them I wouldn't. I said I'd be fine.

BIG MISTAKE #2!

I walked out of the parking lot and into what looked like the set of *Moulin Rouge*. Red velvet walls, model-thin women dressed as flappers, their dates like James Bond. Trapeze artists flew overhead to French music. A catwalk of cobblestone lined with Parisian streetlamps was at the center of it all. And there I was. Dressed like fourteen-year-old Sheridan Spencer— Noble High freshman, sister-mutt.

BIG MISTAKE #3!

I bobbed and weaved through the crowd like a lost kid at Six Flags, searching for Duffy. What was a guy like that doing at a place like this? Did I get the address wrong? Should I call him? Did he call me? I checked my phone. Zero messages. This is all Octavia's fault. If she wasn't having her stupid party Audri would be here. We'd be laughing at that waitress with the cocktail napkin under her stiletto. Instead, I too was stuck where I didn't belong.

I forced myself to do one more lap. Maybe the show would start. Maybe I'd find Duffy. Or the girls he invited from style club. Maybe some casting agent would spot me in my peasant top and hire me to star in *The Sound of Music*.

Then I saw that smart girl Lily from Spanish class. She looked lost too. Only prettier. Much. She was wearing a tight red minidress with pointy black ankle boots and an armload of bangles. Her frizzy dark hair had been ironed and glossed. This was no pear—more like a celery with two perky apples. On Pandora Radio, her station would be J-Lo. Mine would be Maria from *Sesame Street*.

I tapped her on the shoulder. She turned. I said hi. She gasped. I smiled.

What are you doing here? (Lily.)

I was invited.

By whom? (Lily.)

Duffy.

Why?

To see the show.

But—

Where's everyone else?

Who?

The girls from your style club?

What?

Duffy said you were bringing them.

Why would I do that?

I—

Her bottom lip began to twitch.

Do you know where he is? (Lily.)

No. I was just looking for him.

Ican'tbelievethis.

I wondered why she was so upset. And then I knew.

Did you think this was a date?

Her eyes filled with tears. I hoped her mascara was water-proof. My phone rang—

Hold on. (Me, reaching into my clutch.) *This is probably him—*

I answered. It was Octavia. I turned to tell Lily I'd be right back but she was gone.

Hello? (Me, trying to sound cool and not at all curious as to why Octavia would be calling me.) *Hold on, let me go outside, the music is too loud.*

Where are you? (Octavia.)

Who is this? (Ha!)

Octavia.

Who?

Oc-tay-vee-ah!

(Me, snatching the remote away from Sister-Mutt and changing my channel to Paris Hilton.) *Hold on guys, I'm coming. Yes, I'll dance with you. No, my dress is not Dior. It's vintage YSL. Shhh, let me talk. One minute. Sorry, Octavia, what's up? Is it Audri? Is she okay?*

I wanted to see if you were coming tonight.

Where?

My party.

I wasn't invited.

You are now.

Did Audri put you up to this? Because I don't need your charity. I'm at a fashion show with all my—

I'm inviting you because I want you to come. Audri doesn't even know I'm calling.

So why—

This thing between us is stupid. I want to start fresh.

Really? (Me. Wanting to believe her.)

But if you have other—

No, it's okay. Stephan can probably give me a ride. If not I'll ask Matteo. That guy can't say no. Check out his GQ cover, the one with the albino mice, and you'll see what I mean.

Cool. (Octavia.) *So you'll be here soon?*

Yeah.

Oh, Sheridan?

Yeah?

This'll be good.

I poked my head inside and scanned for Duffy one last time. He was nowhere. So I called a taxi and gave the driver Octavia's address.

BIG MISTAKE #4!

To Be Continued . . .

END SCENE.

DUFFY

Friday

Feeling = Over.

The fashion show. My basketball career. My life.

over.

Not a single person showed. Not one. Not even Sister-Mutt.
My whole section was empty. I could have played Rumson. I

wouldn't have had to Wipe. Hud and Coops would still be talking to me. Anton wouldn't be text-threatening me to pay him back. I wouldn't have called the cops on Lily.

Sucks.

Sucks.

Sucks.

Sucks.

Sucks.

Sucks.

Sucks.

Sucks.

My entire life sucks.

Gardner offered me a ride after the show. Only I couldn't deal with him bragging about his commission and talking about the "ahm-bee-ance" like it mattered. So I said no. The whole "affair" was a giant Exxon spill of slickness and I was the oily seagull. I needed to run off the runoff. I didn't care that my house was eight miles from the "venue." I was so pissed I could have gone twenty. I didn't even have earbuds but I ran like I did.

My feet smacked the pavement. My heart pounded. My lungs

stung. The medieval coin necklace smacked against my chest. I didn't care if it retailed for $250 but with the code it could be yours for $105. I ripped it off my neck and whipped it in the bushes on Old Bell Road. I wanted to outrun my feelings. To leave them with the coin and the rest of this night that should never have been mine to begin with. But the horrible feelings stayed with me no matter how fast I ran. So I pumped and worked and pushed until I was too tired to feel anything at all.

Car lights = streaks. Traffic lights = spots. Curbs = cliffs for me to jump off of.

A van rolled up beside me on King's Lane. I figured it was Anton with another lecture on "salesmanship." I sped up. The van did too. "Sexy and I Know It" was blasting inside. Someone rolled down a window. The music became clearer. I didn't want to look. I didn't care who it was or what they wanted. I looked anyway.

It was the Flames driving back from Rumson.

Feeling = Oh no.

I started limping.

Logo with his head out the window: How's that bad ankle treating you?

Feeling = Dizzy. Deaf. Sick.

Hands on my knees, I leaned forward to catch my breath. I begged my Golden "Duffys" to Iron Man me home, but they just stood there, all slick and pathetic, like me.

Feeling = I hate these shoes!

Handfuls of Cheetos were being thrown at me. The guys sped off shouting "Go Flames!"

I ditched my Golden Duffys by the side of the road.

Feeling = I want my mom.

Serious. I actually felt that way. Not that I'd ever admit that to her. I was her son. Not her daughter.

I walked barefoot and thought about Sheridan. We weren't super tight or anything but still. I thought she was real.

Amelia would say: She must have had a good reason for ditching you. Why don't you call and ask if she's okay?

Hud and Coops would call me a wuss if I did that.

Mandy would say: Make her jealous. That's what I do when Gardner takes me for granted. Start with a good outfit. Something that says confidence and curves. Then . . . (yawn = deaf).

Dad would smack me on the back and tell me it's only going to get harder.

Bubbie Libby would tell me to forget about the blonde and focus on the nice Jewish girl next door.

Mom would hug me for a solid hour.

I wanted to listen to Amelia.

I decided if the light at Meyer and Kent Ave. stayed green until I got to the mailbox, I would.

The light turned yellow.

I called Sheridan anyway.

It rang three times before she picked up.

ME: Sheridan?

DUDE: No. It's her boyfriend.

Girls were laughing in the background.

ME: Who is this?

DUDE: It's Logan. Noble Flames MVP. Who's this?

I hung up. I ran the rest of the way barefoot.

The house was dark when I got home.

Feeling = Relieved.

I was too ashamed to see anyone. I wanted to Skype Amelia.

The dogs ran out when I unlocked the door. I chased them all the way to Lily's house. Her parents had just gotten home and hadn't closed the door all the way. The dogs pushed it open and ran inside. Mrs. Bader-Huffman screamed. They bolted up the stairs.

ME: I'm so sorry.

She said it's okay, she was startled, that's all. I was barefoot and smelled like sweat. I hoped she didn't notice.

HER: Where's Lily?

ME: No clue.

Mrs. Bader-Huffman started to freak. She thought Lily and I had plans. Something about a fashion show to raise money for sweatshop workers.

ME: Sweatshop workers?

HER: That's what she told me. You haven't seen her all night?

ME: No. She was supposed to meet me but she never showed.

HER: Oh my god, Alannnnnnn! Lily has been kidnapped!

I did not want to be around for that so I said I'd grab the dogs and go. She was too busy freaking to care.

Me going upstairs: Come, puppies. Come on. (Kissy sound kissy sound.)

I heard their jingling collars in Lily's room.

I walked in all careful, afraid I might see something I'm not supposed to. Like it was the girls' locker room or something. Coops and I dared each other to run through one during our middle school dance and this was nothing like that.

For one thing it didn't smell like shampoo or fruit-flavored gum. It didn't smell like anything girly at all. More like the parts of a library no one hangs in, where the books are old and all about history. There weren't any makeup stains or torn magazines or shoe piles or bright colors like Mandy's. It was more like Amelia's: full maps and encyclopedias and nerdy secrets.

The dogs were scratching the closet like maybe a dead body had been buried in there. I wondered if it was Lily's. Maybe that's why she didn't show up. Maybe her parents murdered her and stuffed her in there. Maybe the dogs heard the whole thing and were trying to tell me. Maybe that's why the Bader-Huffmans were out.

Feeling = Watch your back!

The dogs scratched the Albert Einstein poster right off the door. A picture of Seth from *The O.C.* was hidden underneath. Nerdy secret #1. Called it.

ME: What is it pups?

DOGS: Jingle jingle mwwww mwww woof.

ME: Whatcha got in there?

DOGS: Woof!

277

ME: Bones?

DOGS: A-woof! Woof!

I knocked.

I whispered: Lily?

I knocked again.

I whispered again: Lily? It's Duffy. You in there?

What if she was? Her parents would never let me leave alive. Then again, getting murdered by the Bader-Huffmans might not be so bad. Everyone would like me again and I'd be out of the red with Anton. The timing was ideal.

I checked the hall. I was alone. I gripped the brass knob. I turned it slowly. I swallowed. Everything I did sounded seriously loud. I opened the door. I went blind for a second. Then I opened my eyes.

Nothing. No corpse. No bones. No Lily. Just clothes, another picture of Seth, and a tackle box with a lock. The dogs were still going crazy so I guessed the box was full of unkosher snacks (nerdy secret #2?) because Lily hates being kosher. A label on the back of the lock said "A.D.'s birthday" in tiny font.

Feeling = Same initials as me.

For fun I entered: 12.29.97.

Click.

The lock popped open. I opened the box. I called the cops.

— LATER

Vanessa

October 12th

My arms were slathered in a shedload of Aveeno anti-itch cream. I wasn't expecting fights or poor grades on my first date with Blake. But Mom had just moved back from the hotel and she wanted to give me a ride, so I had to take all necessary precautions.

She told me I looked beautiful[57] and then she started the

---

[57] I did. Lily and I got our hair professionally straightened and had our makeup applied for free by the lady at the Fresh counter. I was lightly dusted, not overdone. I wore a silver long-sleeved dress and black knee-high boots from Steve Madden. Dad nearly passed out.

engine and cried. She wanted to talk about why she had been gone so long but I shut her down. I refused to spend my first date scratching like a flea-ridden cat. I had waited seven days for her explanation. What was one more day? So I said that and then blasted the radio. "Sexy and I Know It" was on.[58]

A letter in a plain white envelope rested on the seat between us. It was addressed to me in Helvetica 12-point font.

"What's this?"

"Oh, that came today," she said, sniffling. "I forgot to give it to you."

"Finally," I said, assuming it was U.S. Customs saying my SWAP bracelets had cleared. If I collected the money by Wednesday I'd still have time to enter and I wouldn't need "the solution" again until finals.

I tore the letter open. The note was brief. Helvetica 12-point all caps:

I KNEW YOU WERE UP TO SOMETHING.
NOW I HAVE PROOF. YOU'RE DONE.

My vision blurred. I read it four more times anyway. My forehead began to sweat. The moisture was making my straightened hair curl.

Who did this? Who knows my secret? What did they want from me? A confession? Surrender? Expulsion?

----

[58] Perfect.

"Nessa, are you okay?" Mom asked. "Did you eat something?"

"What?" I snapped, desperate to be alone with my panic.

"Something's wrong. I can tell. Is it the letter?"

"No," I said, crumpling it up. "Just an announcement about gluten-free Girl Scout cookies."

"Well, you don't look okay."

"Thanks, Mom, just what every girl wants to hear on her way to a party."

"That's not what I meant."

We rode the rest of the way in silence. Ver? I didn't want to go on my date anymore. I needed to know who sent this note and why.

A.J. knew my secret but he would never turn me in. Especially since I upgraded him to a C+. There weren't any security cameras in the office when I snuck in. And Lily is the only person I told....

FOE NO YOU DIZN'T!

How could I have been so stupid?

Deepak teaches us to follow our instincts and honor our inner voice. From day one that voice told me to watch out for her in two languages.[59] This is obviously about Blake. I mean, how can a girl spend that much time with a guy that perfect and not fall in love? She can't. It defies chemistry, logic, and love.

---

[59] English and Creole.

I should have known Lily was in denial of her feelings. Mine must have woken hers up. Now she sees me as a threat. But, come on. My kind of threat and the one she just mailed to me are unequivocally unequal.

Mom stopped the car in front of Octavia's. Blake was by the window talking up a group of girls. He said something and they all laughed. I ached with jealousy. I'll never laugh again, because juvenile detention centers aren't funny.

I had plans to meet Lily on the roof of the school in an hour. We were going to fix her grades. I wanted to go straight there and confront her but she was at a fashion show with Duffy. I would have called but she didn't own a phone. I would have sent a letter by carrier pigeon but my hands were too shaky to write. Who else knows about this????

I forced myself to kiss my mother[60] goodbye and then I forced myself to go inside. Logan from the basketball team was talking to Octavia, Audri, and the Orphan about some joyride he took with Sheridan Spencer. Octavia was teasing him, saying he liked Sheridan. That it had nothing to do with the car and that he really wanted to ride Sheridan. Logan disagreed. Octavia said, then why did you go?

Logan said, any guy would say yes to an M3 GTR!

This made Octavia squeal with joy. I froze.

"Did you say you rode an M3 with Sheridan Spencer?" I

---

[60] Still angry.

283

asked. "As in Spencer BMW?"

"Hey, Vanessa," Octavia said. "Awesome hair."

Audri agreed. Then she whispered something in Jagger the Orphan's ear, he nodded, and they took off giggling.

"Thanks," I said to Octavia even though my eyes were still on Logan. He looked like a boy-band kind of guy. "Logan, did you really ride an M3 with Sheridan?"

"He did," Octavia answered for him. "Not because he likes her, though. He was using her for the car."

"When was this?" I asked. "Last Friday?"

"Think so," Logan said, crushing a handful of chips and sprinkling them in Octavia's hair. This cracked her up. She dumped the bowl on his head.

Me, about to start crying. "Did you lose a Noble High key chain that night?"

This got his attention. "Yeah, and a Hugo Boss jacket. Did you find them?"

I was too stunned to answer. A.J. was innocent! I wanted to punch Logan and hug him at the same time.

The front door opened. It was Sheridan Spencer.

"Hey, welcome," Octavia purred. "Love the vintage dress."[61]

"Hey," Sheridan said. She ignored the dress comment and

....

 and some *Sound of Music* top. Hardly a vintage hardly smart so I let it go.

focused on Logan's arm, which was resting on Octavia's shoulder.

"You know my date, right?" Octavia asked.

"I thought you had a game tonight?" Sheridan said.

"He did," Octavia said. "I invited him to come after."

"Is this why you invited me here?" Sheridan asked. "To rub it in my face?"

Octavia smirked. "He's not your boyfriend, Sheridan. I just wanted you to see that."

"Boyfriend?" Logan said. "Who said anything about a boyfriend?"

"She did," Octavia said.

"I did not!"

Sheridan's phone rang. The screen flashed DUFFY. Logan grabbed it before she could talk. Sheridan fought to get it back. Octavia was laughing. I stood there feeling like an extra in a teen movie.

Sheridan had her hands full with those two unequivocally vapid morons. So I decided to check in with Blake and then circle back to ask her about the joyride that ruined my brother's life.

When I got to the living room Blake was gone. Caprice Simmons said he got a call from Lily and took off. He left through the garage because he didn't want to be rude. Then she went on about how cute and considerate he is and how lucky Lily was to have him.

"Have him?"

"Yeah, as her boyfriend."

"How do you know they're together?" I asked.

"He told me," she said.

I said something nasty in Creole and went to the bathroom. I sat on the seat and cried. Then I got angry and stopped.

Lily felt threatened so she set me up. Now I would take her down. I dialed the police to report a possible hacking at Noble High. Then I went to find Sheridan.

Don't get mad, get even.

—Robert F. Kennedy

Jagger

Oct. 12.

I pick Audri up on my bike and we double to Octavia's party. I
ride right through the puddles and I don't even care.

She looks cuter than Ghoulia from *Monster High*.

She says my fedora is fedorable. We laugh.

We are hanging out and having fun.

At one point she whispers, are we gonna do this or what?

My face turns red even though I'm not exactly sure what she
means by this.

Depends.

On what?

What does it rhyme with? I ask.

Bake trout, she says.

I say sure.

I have never baked trout before but she doesn't know this and I don't want her to.

She takes my hand. Hers is clammy too. Normally a girl with a clammy hand makes me kind of sick but hers makes me feel better. Was this her first time too?

I follow her. Everything inside me speeds.

A few older guys are sitting on the landing at the top of the steps.

They are drinking from red plastic cups.

I can tell they don't go to Noble because they are all pierced and tatted up and Noble doesn't allow that.

I get closer. I stop. I freak. One of the guys has a tattoo of an electric chair on his arm. I know that tattoo. I know that arm. I check the face. It's him.

I have to get out of there before he sees me. Before he gives me away. I say baking trout will have to wait.

I run down the steps.

Audri asks me what's wrong.

I say Crazy Pat, the navy SEAL.

She tells me to hurry before I get caught. She's right.

Only it's not Crazy Pat I'm worried about. He's not real.

Nothing I told Audri is. Everything has been a lie and she almost found out. That's what really scares me.

-J

Lily

Friday, October 12, 2012

It was cold and dark and my butt hurt from sitting on a skateboard for two hours. My red dress was smeared with snot and my temples throbbed.

Blake clambered up to my side on the school roof. He took a hit off his inhaler and said, "How was your date?"

"Awful."

"I knew that guy had Coxsackie," Blake said, pulling me into his chest for a hug.

I was crying too hard to laugh.

"He invited Sheridan. He invited the entire style club. It wasn't even a date. He doesn't like me. I'm too weird. I spent my computer money on masculine Euro clothes for a guy who thinks I'm weird."

"That's not true. I'm the only one who thinks you're weird. Did he say you looked hot, because you do, Lil. You really look—"

"He didn't even see me. I saw Sheridan and took off."

"Why did you—"

"I can't compete with that. She didn't even attempt to look pretty. She just showed up in jeans, a hippie top, and a messy ponytail. Like she was so confident she didn't have to try. I hate blondes. I hate blondes more than I hate homeschool. And I hate homeschool more than anything and I'm going to have to go back if—where's Vanessa? Why isn't she here?"

"I left the party before she got there."

"Blake!" I punched his arm. "Why?"

"You called me collect. You were crying. I started wheezing. I thought you had been jumped."

"I called you because I don't know Vanessa's cell phone number. I called collect because I didn't have a quarter. Blake, why did you ditch her? You're messing everything up."

"I thought you were in trouble."

"I am now," I said, crying for a whole new reason. "She's going to think you stood her up. Now she won't come. My mom is going to see my real grades. I'm gonna be a Homie again!"

"Shhhh." Blake pulled me closer. I thought he was trying to comfort me but he was being literal. "Hear that?" Police sirens wailed on the street below. They were getting louder. "What's going on?"

"Who cares." I sighed and rested my head on his belly. I searched the sky for shooting stars but it was full of clouds. No surprise there.

Lily Bader-Huffman

EPILOGUE

Hello, Reader.

What do you think of our Noble heroes so far? Lies, betrayal, unrequited love, jealousy, cheating, and stealing. "Outstanding," aren't we? Of course, I'm being facetious. Or am I?

The Phoenix Five did manage to hide their true selves and convince their classmates that they had it all. How did they do it?

That's the outstanding part.

To be continued...

X

Acknowledgments

You know the expression "It takes a village"? Well, this is where I'm supposed to thank the members of my village for helping me bring this novel to life. But in this particular case, there was no village. I am 100 percent responsible for the making of *Pretenders*. I didn't need anyone or anything. Not even a fancy machine to print the books. I typed every copy myself. I illustrated millions of covers, and I corrected my own grammatical errors. I negotiated the deal; I was my own assistant. I drove the eighteen-wheelers that delivered the books to the stores, and then I stocked the shelves while you slept.

You're welcome.

Lisi

(If I were a Pretender.)

But I'm not. So keep reading, please.

Acknowledgments (for Real)

I'm far too grateful to the following villagers to have pulled that off. Here's why:

My editor, Erin Stein: She let me pitch this over the phone, which was huge because I can't stand writing up my ideas. I didn't know who the characters were, but she trusted me and told me to go for it. I did. Then she helped me make it so much better. TPTPTP!

Copy master: Barbara Bakowski. This woman IS the English language.
Design: Liz Casal, Sasha Illingworth, and David Caplan
Marketing: Andrew Smith and Mara Lander
PR: Melanie Chang and Kristina Aven

My agent Richard Abate: Brilliant adviser. Fierce negotiator. Loyal friend. Incredible hair. FUPM.
His assistant, Melissa Kahn: She always has the answers.
My fancy LA attorney, Alex Kohner: We laugh. We cry. I sign. Thank you for always caring.
His associate Logan Clare: Smart. Funny. Best voice ever.

My editorial assistant, Alisha Maddocks: Alisha refers to herself as my "office elf," but no elf could do what this girl does. (That's right, Santa, I said it.) I am endlessly grateful for all she does and everything she teaches me. She has incredible hair, too.

Gorjana and Vanessa S. from gorjana & griffin, for helping me create the real SWAP. Want one? www.gorjana-griffin.com. And to my amazing friend Mary Beth Pugh, for bringing us together.

JJ Hutcheon, for reading—and finishing—my first draft. SOL.

Candace Brokenshire: She always finds my air.

The Fugate girls: Christine, Caterina, and Sara—my Laguna Beach focus group.

Nick Alexander Imports BMW and MINI: Thanks for advising me on all things BMW-related. (Can I please have a MINI now?)

The regulars on LisiHarrison.com: Thank you for always showing up.

Immeasurable amounts of gratitude go to Kevy, Luke, Jess, and Bee-Bee. You are my heart. To Mom and Dad. To the Gottliebs, Coopers, and Harrisons. And to my amazing friends. Thanks to each one of you for letting me slip into the cone of silence. You let me go and you welcome me back. Thirty-one times and counting...

I'm off to write book two. Monkey paws, don't fail me now.

Find out what the
Pretenders do next...

Three girls, two guys,
and five secret journals

LICENSE
TO
SPILL

A PRETENDERS NOVEL
BY #1 NEW YORK TIMES BESTSELLING AUTHOR
LISI HARRISON

Available now!